Resolved

The Queen's Alpha Series, Volume 12

W.J. May

Published by Dark Shadow Publishing, 2019.

This is a work of fiction. Similarities to real people, places, or events are entirely coincidental.

RESOLVED

First edition. July 15, 2019.

Copyright © 2019 W.J. May.

Written by W.J. May.

Also by W.J. May

Bit-Lit Series
Lost Vampire
Cost of Blood
Price of Death

Blood Red Series
Courage Runs Red
The Night Watch
Marked by Courage
Forever Night
The Other Side of Fear

Daughters of Darkness: Victoria's Journey
Victoria
Huntress
Coveted (A Vampire & Paranormal Romance)
Twisted
Daughter of Darkness - Victoria - Box Set

Alpha's Permission
Blood Bonding
Oracle of Nightmares
Shadows in the Night
Paranormal Huntress BOX SET #1-3

Prophecy Series
Only the Beginning
White Winter
Secrets of Destiny

The Chronicles of Kerrigan
Rae of Hope
Dark Nebula
House of Cards
Royal Tea
Under Fire
End in Sight
Hidden Darkness
Twisted Together
Mark of Fate
Strength & Power
Last One Standing
Rae of Light
The Chronicles of Kerrigan Box Set Books # 1 - 6

The Chronicles of Kerrigan: Gabriel
Living in the Past

Present For Today
Staring at the Future

The Chronicles of Kerrigan Prequel
Christmas Before the Magic
Question the Darkness
Into the Darkness
Fight the Darkness
Alone in the Darkness
Lost in Darkness
The Chronicles of Kerrigan Prequel Series Books #1-3

The Chronicles of Kerrigan Sequel
A Matter of Time
Time Piece
Second Chance
Glitch in Time
Our Time
Precious Time

The Hidden Secrets Saga
Seventh Mark (part 1 & 2)

The Kerrigan Kids
School of Potential

The Queen's Alpha Series
Eternal
Everlasting
Unceasing
Evermore
Forever
Boundless
Prophecy
Protected
Foretelling
Revelation
Betrayal
Resolved

The Senseless Series
Radium Halos - Part 1
Radium Halos - Part 2
Nonsense
Perception

Standalone
Shadow of Doubt (Part 1 & 2)
Five Shades of Fantasy
Shadow of Doubt - Part 1
Shadow of Doubt - Part 2
Four and a Half Shades of Fantasy
Dream Fighter
What Creeps in the Night

Forest of the Forbidden
Arcane Forest: A Fantasy Anthology
The First Fantasy Box Set

Watch for more at www.wjmaybooks.com.

THE QUEEN'S ALPHA SERIES

RESOLVED

USA Today Bestselling Author
W . J . M A Y

Copyright 2019 by W.J. May

Have You Read the C.o.K Series?

The Chronicles of Kerrigan
Book I - *Rae of Hope* is FREE!

BOOK TRAILER:

http://www.youtube.com/watch?v=gILAwXxx8MU

How hard do you have to shake the family tree to find the truth about the past?

Fifteen year-old Rae Kerrigan never really knew her family's history. Her mother and father died when she was young and it is only when she accepts a scholarship to the prestigious Guilder Boarding School in England that a mysterious family secret is revealed.

Will the sins of the father be the sins of the daughter?

As Rae struggles with new friends, a new school and a star-struck forbidden love, she must also face the ultimate challenge: receive a tattoo on her sixteenth birthday with specific powers that may bind her to an unspeakable darkness. It's up to Rae to undo the dark evil in her family's past and have a ray of hope for her future.

Find W.J. May

Website:
https://www.wjmaybooks.com
Facebook:
https://www.facebook.com/pages/Author-WJ-May-FAN-PAGE/
141170442608149
Newsletter:
SIGN UP FOR W.J. May's Newsletter to find out about new releases,
updates, cover reveals and even freebies!
http://eepurl.com/97aYf

Resolved Blurb:

U SA Today Bestselling author, W.J. May, continues the highly antici-
pated bestselling YA/NA series about love, betrayal, magic and fantasy. Be prepared to fight, it's the only option.

Who do you hold on to when the sky begins to fall?

When an ancient curse takes hold of the land, Katerina Damaris
and her friends are forced to do the impossible. Venture into the belly
of the beast.

Trapped in a wasteland at the end of the world, they find themselves facing dangers they could never have imagined. Old enemies and
resurrected monsters. An army of darkness like never before.

The gang races to unlock the prophecy, but before the secret is un-
veiled one of their party is taken before their very eyes.

The field is primed. The players are ready.

A single match, and the whole thing will go up in flames...

She will fight for what is hers.

BE CAREFUL WHO YOU trust. Even the devil was once an angel.

The Queen's Alpha Series

Eternal
Everlasting
Unceasing
Evermore
Forever
Boundless
Prophecy
Protected
Foretelling
Revelation
Betrayal
Resolved

COMING SOON!

The Omega Queen Series

Discipline
Bravery
Courage
Conquer
Strength
Validation

Chapter 1

Nathaniel Fell.

All her life it seemed, Katerina had been searching for the man—whether she knew it or not. The secret puppet-master. The one pulling all the strings. Considering how much she'd heard about him from the others, considering how much time he'd spent haunting her dreams...

...the man didn't disappoint.

He had to be over seven feet tall, towering over the rest of them and holding Dylan like he was some sort of doll. His hands were scarred but steady. There wasn't a speck of color in his eyes.

In a different time, he might have been handsome. If his life had turned out the way it was supposed to, the way everyone else had needed it to, things might have been different. There was a regal cast to his features that was not unbecoming. A strong bearing that came from years of carrying a sword. But time had eroded everything that might have once been good about him, leaving nothing but the wasted shell underneath.

"Come on, say something." He spoke to no one in particular, rewarding everyone in the cave with the same jaunty smile. "So long we've been waiting for this moment, surely you have something to say." His eyes fell on each of them in turn. "Tanya, Aidan—anything?"

They startled, but said nothing. Both looked terrified he knew their names.

"What about you, love?" His eyes fell on Katerina, who stood mute, before travelling over her shoulder to where Cassiel had pushed shakily to his feet. "You?"

The fae's lips parted but he merely stood there, as if he'd wandered into a dream.

"*You* had better keep quiet," the Knight teased Dylan lightly. "Try to speak, and I'm afraid this dagger is going to sink right into your throat."

The ranger hadn't moved an inch since freezing in the blinding flash of light, then being yanked straight off his feet. A massive arm was wrapped around the front of his chest, holding him with such force that he found himself actually leaning back into the Knight, pressing his head into his bulky shoulder. Anything to avoid the blade.

"What a disappointment!" The knight chuckled to himself, clucking his tongue with a condescending smile. "*This* is the best the fates have to offer? I was hoping for more."

Now would have been a great time to whip out some one-liner. A scathing burn to silence the man and wipe that insufferable smile from his face. But the friends had nothing.

Aidan. Katerina spoke telepathically instead, keeping her eyes locked on the Knight. *Can you speak with Dylan or hear his thoughts? Can you get to him in time?*

They were bonded now, so it wasn't an unreasonable assumption. But the vampire hesitated only a moment before discreetly shaking his head.

The Knight didn't miss a thing.

"Ah yes, I remember that. The blood bond." His voice softened, almost wistfully, as he shifted the hand with the blade. "We'd bonded as well—the five of us. There's nothing quite like it."

Katerina stifled a shudder, staring at him in the dim light. Yes, he'd bonded with the rest of them. Lived their every happiness, fought their every enemy. Faced their every fear.

Then he'd thrusted a sword into his lover's back.

"Let him go."

She hadn't planned on speaking. Truth be told, she was surprised she had the strength. Not that it came out very loud—a mere whisper in the dark.

The Knight turned his attention to her, tightening his grip on Dylan at the same time. "Is this the one you've chosen?" he asked with mild curiosity. "It seems inevitable that some of you would fall in love."

There was a sudden movement as Dylan strained against the hands holding him, only for the tip of the dagger to press into his skin. A soft cry died on his lips. Then he was quiet once more.

Katerina's eyes widened as she took an involuntary step forward. "Please...take me instead."

It was her pendant he was after. Her bloodline that had been so closely tied to his own. If she and her friends were fated to replace the old members of the prophecy, then it was her destiny to replace him. Surely that was a better offer.

"Please," she whispered, extending a willing hand.

There was a streak of color in the darkness, a flash of pale skin and dark hair. A second later she was right back where she started, imprisoned in Aidan's inescapable arms.

And then came the laughter...it never really stopped.

"Yes, that love is all over you. Both of you." He twisted the knife almost playfully, smiling as Dylan's back arched in pain. "I remember that as well. That feeling."

There was a sudden movement on the other side of the cavern as Cassiel took a compulsive step forward. He might have shaken the wizard's spell, but the damage was already done. While the others were already pushed to the brink with lack of food and water, he had been magically pushed three days more. His lips were cracked and bleeding. The hollows of his cheeks were almost gaunt.

"And *you*...look terribly familiar." The Knight's eyes glittered in the dark, fastening on to the pale and trembling Prince of the Fae. "Like the woman I used to love. An immortal queen."

Eliea.

The fabled Queen of the Fae who had died in Laurelwood Forest—trapping the Knight inside with her. Cursing the man who'd killed her, the same man to whom she'd given her heart.

Cassiel trembled once, but stood tall. "She was my aunt."

The man nodded slowly, as if he'd already been told that piece of information several years before. His eyes swept over the fae for a moment before tightening with that wistful smile.

"Your aunt..." He paused, amending whatever he'd been going to say as an image of her lovely face flashed through his mind. "...should have known better than to trust me."

It was a good thing Cassiel was starving. Because if he'd been able to reach the Knight, he surely would have been killed. As it stood, he merely swept forward a few steps then fell suddenly to his knees, breathless and glaring, unable to push to his feet.

The Knight watched him a moment, taking another long look at his face. "But you...you don't look much younger than me."

How he could possibly tell, Katerina had no idea. Her friend might have been almost five hundred years old, but to the rest of the world he appeared nineteen.

Cassiel simply stared back at him, eyes burning with rage.

"You were there?" the Knight asked curiously.

Taviel. They have to be talking about Taviel.

"I think I remember you," the Knight murmured, sensing that Cassiel would be either unable or unwilling to answer. "At the burning at the citadel." His eyes clouded over, lost in years gone by. "You refused to leave, were trying to save someone...*pieces* of someone..." He looked up suddenly, remembering the prince's face. "They had to carry you out of the city."

This time, the memory was too much.

Cassiel threw himself forward with a mighty cry, forcing Aidan to release Katerina just to catch him in time. She darted to Dylan, only to freeze, staring into those beautiful captive eyes. A second later, she found herself looking up without permission at the man with the blade.

He saw her watching, decided to give her a little demonstration.

With a wicked smirk, he tightened his grip and twisted his hand. Digging the tip of the knife into Dylan's throat as the ranger's feet dangled helplessly above the ground. He let out a broken gasp, grabbing the blade itself before jerking back with a sudden cry of pain.

"What the hell is that?!"

The others stopped their struggle, staring up in alarm.

The second the blade touched his skin it had darkened to a kind of shadow, one that rippled like water in the dim light. Little wisps of smoke rose out from it and the edges charred over with a soot-like stain, creeping over the metal like a recently extinguished flame.

Dylan shook his hands, oblivious to the added pain it caused, almost as if he could shake any of the lingering shadow away from his skin. The Knight watched impassively before again pressing the blade to his neck, holding him prisoner once more.

"That, my child, is what we call a *doronos*. A cursed blade." It gleamed slightly in the shadowy light, almost as if it was listening. "Able to bewitch whomever it pierces."

Dylan's eyes were screaming, but his body had gone very still.

It was a word they had learned as children, whispered in deliberately frightening voices in a bedtime story by the governess or maid. Katerina had always assumed it was fiction, but in the last year she'd come to challenge that word quite a bit. Still, she could never have imagined...

"Would you like to see how it feels?"

In a flash, Dylan dropped to the floor of the cave—released from the massive arms that had imprisoned him. The vampire's blood had healed all wounds, but his body was still weak from hunger and he struggled to find his balance—spinning around as the Knight circled him in the dark.

"Stop it!" Katerina shrieked, racing forward once more. "Just leave him alone! He isn't the one you're looking for!"

A trembling hand caught the edge of her cloak and pulled her back. Tanya might have been just as weak as the others, but she was still stronger that Katerina. And there was no way she was going to let one of her best friends offer herself up to a cursed blade.

"Let go!" the queen commanded, striking back at her. "I said LET GO!"

Cassiel was in a similar frenzy, fighting hard against the vampire. But in his present condition, he was no match. And even if he'd reached them, there would be nothing he could do.

The Knight ignored all of them, focused only on his prize.

"That's true," he agreed quietly, circling the ranger like a cat toying with its prey, "I wasn't coming for him. I was coming for you. But now that I'm here..."

In a flash of speed he flew forward.

...and pierced the ranger with the enchanted blade.

Dylan let out a gasp as it slid into the skin beneath his collarbone. At first, he looked merely surprised. Then angry, then afraid. But before he could do a thing to stop it the Knight pushed it in further, burying it all the way to the hilt and rendering him completely helpless.

"Dylan!"

Katerina's scream echoed in the cave, but the ranger couldn't hear her.

A strange paleness swept over this skin. His damp locks of hair trembled for a moment, then went very still. When the knife twisted ever so slightly, he let out a quiet moan.

"For centuries I've been waiting," the Knight whispered, watching the subtle transformation flickering over the young man's face. "Keeping to the shadows, biding my time until the prophecy came to life anew... I'm not ready for it to be over just yet."

The knife jerked a final time and Dylan cried out. His head bowed, dark hair spilling forward. He reached out blindly, steadying his hands on the man's chest.

Nathaniel caught him with a smile, patting the back of his head.

"I've decided to keep him."

Upon those words the magic of the dagger swept over him, doing its deadly work. That ashen tint was spreading, working its way into every corner, erasing the usual shine. Arms and legs had ceased to have any feeling. The darkness of the cave was suddenly awash with unholy light.

His body tensed and shuddered.

"Shh..." Nathanial whispered. "Let it happen. Open up to it." His eyes locked with Katerina's as he circled behind Dylan, whispering in his ear. "Embrace it."

Dylan.

Never had she seen such an expression. Not on him, not on anyone. There was something inhuman about it. As if he'd progressed to different levels of pain.

There was one final cry then he fell forward, catching onto the Knight without realizing it, clinging tightly as tears ran down his face. Another sting of pain rushed through him, punishing any resistance, and he let out a broken gasp, pressing his forehead into the man's shoulder.

"No more..." he panted breathlessly. "Please...I can't..."

The others tried to run forward. They had been trying to run forward for some time. But that dark light had frozen them, just as surely as it had overtaken their friend. Leaving them with nothing to do but watch powerlessly as the Knight reached down and lifted his chin.

"Just a little longer... take a breath." He spoke almost gently, staring appraisingly. Then, all at once, he brightened with a sudden smile. "*There.*"

Katerina didn't know if she'd ever been more terrified. In a kind of daze she watched as the man she loved slowly turned around, no longer needing the Knight's supporting arms. At a glance, there was nothing different. Nothing that would indicate the tragedy that had come to pass.

But his eyes told a different story. There was no light in those eyes.

"DYLAN!"

She didn't know if she screamed it out loud, or only in her head. Either way, it didn't seem to matter. The love of her life was gone now. In a place where she couldn't follow.

"Come."

Without a backwards glance the Knight headed out of the cave, into the sunlight just beyond. Without a backwards glance, the ranger followed.

As if this wasn't the man he'd sworn to kill.

As if his friends weren't screaming, out of their minds.

They vanished through the opening just as the darkness lifted and the friends were finally able to move. They streaked after them without a second's pause...only to screech to a sudden stop.

"Get back!"

Cassiel grabbed Katerina just as a pair of massive jaws swooped out of the sky, snapping in the air right where she'd been standing. With a reflexive cry the friends reversed their momentum, leaping back the way they'd come just as a beast landed before them.

A beast unlike anything they had ever seen.

Too big to be real, too frightening for them not to be dreaming, it landed on the ground in front of them—quaking the very foundations of the earth as several stones piled near the front of the cave rattled and fell. They fell themselves a second later, instinctually covering their heads as a pair of enormous wings swept over them, scraping their backs as it took to flight.

A dragon? Katerina lifted her head a few inches, staring through her fingers as the beast threw back its head with an unearthly cry. *Is that some kind of dragon?*

She wanted to say yes, but there were things she couldn't account for. First there was the sheer, unparalleled size. Then there were the three snapping heads.

But all of that paled compared to what she saw next.

The man she'd vowed to marry...sitting on the beast's back.

He didn't look down at her, didn't say a word. The Knight flashed his signature smile, but the ranger stared ahead blankly. Seeing without seeing, hands wrapped around the deadly spikes.

There was another gust of wind, one strong enough to knock Tanya off her feet, then they shot straight up into the sky—aiming for the distant horizon. Leaving the cave behind.

"DYLAN!"

There was time for one more try. One final scream. Then they disappeared into the blinding sunlight. The last thing Katerina saw were those lifeless eyes vanishing into the clouds.

Chapter 2

This cannot be real. This cannot be happening.

Katerina stared without blinking at the crystal sky. Just moments ago, there had been a dark layer of clouds. A cyclone that descended from nowhere, churning around in stark defiance to the still-blinding sunlight. Now, it was as if that had never happened. When the dragon vanished it took the storm with it. Leaving nothing but innocent sunshine and a ringing silence in its wake.

"Dylan." She whispered his name, like at any moment he might reappear.

Stranger things had happened. It would be no stranger than the fact that he'd left in the first place. That he'd climbed atop that terrifying monster and vanished on the morning breeze.

There was a scuffle behind her. The rustling sound of fabric slipping on stone. She heard, but didn't see it as Tanya fell. Heard, but didn't see the gasp of pain that followed. The way Aidan carefully pulled open the back of her shirt, revealing the deep gash the dragon wing had left behind.

A dragon? Is that what it was?

Katerina still didn't know. Considering everything else that had happened, it seemed the least of their problems. But here she was, wondering anyway. Staring in astonishment at the open sky.

"Are you all right?"

The vampire was in front of her now, dark eyes staring down in concern as she tilted her face to the sun. Even standing directly in front of her he was unable to capture her gaze, unable to break through the breathless trance that had taken hold of her.

"Kat?"

Where were they going? Back to the Dunes? It was a long journey from the High Kingdom, but on the back of such a beast there was a chance it would only take a few days, a few hours.

"Katerina, say something to me. Please."

A few days, a few hours. Could Dylan hold on for that long? Wasn't the cursed knife still buried in his shoulder? I didn't see the Knight take it out...

A violent shudder rocked her shoulders, shaking her where she stood.

Never in a thousand years could she forget what happened, never could she pry the ghastly image from her mind: Dylan, falling forward. Nathaniel, catching him with gentle hands.

She didn't know if the ranger could stay up on his own. She didn't know if he'd succumb to blood loss, or exhaustion, or hunger long before they arrived. But somehow she didn't think the Knight was going to let him fall. She had the worst feeling he'd be handled with velvet gloves.

That's what you do with your playthings. You handle them with great care.

"Katerina—*please!*"

There was a touch of panic now in Aidan's voice, but the queen never heard it. The world could be burning down around her, but she'd never take her eyes away from that crystal clear sky.

At any rate, she hadn't yet asked herself the most important question.

Can it be undone?

Up until recently, she hadn't had much experience in the world of magic. But she knew a dark enchantment when she saw one. From the second that blade pierced his skin Dylan had been bewitched, through and through. Yes, he'd tried to fight it. But it wasn't something you could fight. A *doronos* consumed completely, burning away every remnant of what you'd been before. Every thought and feeling. Leaving nothing but a hollow shell, to be filled with the will of someone else.

At least, that's what the storybooks say. But who knows if you can—

A sharp crack flung her head to the side, followed by sudden burst of pain.

She lifted a hand to her cheek, blinking rapidly, only to see Cassiel standing directly in front of her—looking as though that *doronos* had burned him as well. He offered two words in apology.

"Wake up."

The trance fell away as reality settled in hard and fast. All at once the sky wasn't twinkling with innocent sunshine, it was *scorching* hot. Suddenly the lack of clouds didn't indicate the loss of a dragon, but spoke to a consequence that had the potential to be equally severe.

We don't have any food. Any water.

And it's a three-day journey to the nearest town.

The shape-shifter and the fae were already in critical shape. When the wizard had died, his spell died with him. But not before he'd sped up their symptoms. Starvation for one, thirst for another. Neither was reversible. Neither was something they could possibly survive.

It's up to me, Katerina realized with sudden clarity. *I'm the only chance we've got.*

"Yeah, I'm just...sorry." She blinked again, hyper aware that three sets of eyes were still fastened upon her every breath. "Let me just shift and we'll-we'll find some water, and then..."

She didn't understand why they weren't moving. Why they were staring with such pity in their eyes. Then her hand drifted to her forehead. It pulled away wet with blood.

Her knees gave out a second later and she fell into Aidan's arms.

The world was spinning. She didn't know whether it was the delirium, the blood loss, or the shock of seeing her boyfriend carried off into the sky, but she couldn't seem to catch her breath.

"I'll just shift," she whispered, clinging to his sleeve, "then every-thing will be okay. We can find water on the way—food for Tanya. That-that dragon was really big, so we'll be able to see where it's going. We'll be able to follow it."

Aidan shared a quick look with Cassiel, then his face tightened in pain. "Honey—"

"I know I probably can't beat it, but I can at least distract it for a while." She was speaking more rapidly now, completely unaware that she'd started trembling. "Maybe long enough that you guys can grab Dylan and get somewhere safe."

Why were they looking at her like that? Why weren't they helping?

"Just stop talking for a second," Aidan said quietly. "You need to—"

"No, *listen*," she cut him off swiftly. "I know it looked bad, but he'll be fine once that knife gets out of him. All you need to do is pull it out of his—"

"Katerina," Cassiel interjected this time, glancing back at the cave. "...look."

She stared at him a moment, stilling with an unnamed dread, be-fore turning around to follow his gaze. There was something lying in the mouth of the cave, gleaming as it caught the morning light. It only took her a second to realize what it was.

Then the world came crashing down.

"No!"

The blade.

She was back in Aidan's arms a moment later, weeping uncontrol-lably as she grabbed fistfuls of his coat. The others had already seen it. They'd almost tripped over it as they'd sprinted outside. They couldn't bring themselves to look at it a second longer, but she couldn't tear her eyes away. She stretched up in the vampire's lap, staring breathlessly over his shoulder.

Cassiel took one look at her, then walked away.

"This isn't going to work," he said under his breath.

As he stumbled to the ground by his girlfriend's side Aidan turned to Katerina entreatingly, taking her face between his hands and forcing her to look into his eyes.

"Honey, listen to me for a second... Can you shift?"

Her breath caught in her chest as a trickle of blood spilled down the side of her face. In an instant, she realized *that* was the real question. Everything else would have to wait.

There was no hope of finding Dylan if they couldn't get off the mountain. And unless she could shift, there was no way of getting off the mountain before they starved.

"Yes, I..." She trailed off, then pushed weakly to her feet. He steadied her. "I'm sure that I can shift. Just give me a second to..."

But she couldn't shift. She couldn't stand—none of them could. Dylan had lost the ability to transform into a wolf before they'd even reached the cave. They'd been too worn down from just finding the wizard, let alone after the damage had happened inside.

"Stand back," she commanded bravely, trying to pull her arm free. "You'll be crushed if you're standing too close when it happens. I'm going to need a little—"

She fell to her knees before she could finish the sentence.

"—space."

It was no use. She knew it the second she hit the ground. The others had suspected it from the moment they left the cave, bleeding freely with the sun scorching down on their heads.

"You'll have to go," Cassiel said softly.

Katerina lifted her head to see him staring at Aidan, a look of quiet resignation in his eyes. A silent look passed between them, then the vampire shook his head.

"If I leave, you'll have no one to protect you." His dark eyes darted around the desolate landscape, flickering back to the cave. "Anything could come out of these woods. You wouldn't—"

"There isn't anything in the woods," Cassiel interrupted quietly. "That's the problem. If there was something here we'd have eaten it long ago."

"Cass—"

"The only thing we *need* is food and water, Aidan. And the only person who has a chance of finding it in time is you. I can't go, neither can Tanya. Katerina would fall right out of the sky."

It wasn't often the men disagreed. Usually because they were most often right. Aidan didn't disagree with Cassiel now, and yet he couldn't bring himself to leave them all alone.

"What if I don't make it back in time?" he whispered. "What if I—"

"—what if you're not here to say goodbye?"

Cassiel finished the vampire's question softly, his eyes softening with a faint smile. It wasn't like him to speak so grimly in front of his girlfriend—the man was protective to a fault. But Tanya was past the point of listening. Her eyes were closed and her head was in his lap. If there was ever a time to save them, save *all* of them, the vampire would have to leave that very moment.

"Then it's been a pleasure, Aidan." The fae lifted his hand shakily in between them. "And I wouldn't change a thing."

The vampire stared down at him for a moment before taking his hand.

"...except maybe this."

Cassiel laughed weakly, tightening his grip.

"Yeah, on second thought, there are a few things I would change."

Aidan stared at him for another moment, trying his best to smile, before kneeling down and kissing the forehead of the sleeping girl beside him. His hand lingered on her spiky hair, smoothing it unnecessarily, before he slowly turned around to face the fire-haired girl with the teary eyes.

"Kat—"

Don't say anything.

She spoke only within the confines of her head, knowing he was still able to hear. Instead of a protracted farewell, one that would surely tear her shredded heart into even smaller pieces, she reached behind her neck and grabbed the tiny golden chain.

"Here, take this." She slipped off the ruby pendant and held it in the air between them. "If there's really a chance we're going to die up here, at least it will be with someone safe."

It's not a matter of chance. We are *going to die up here.*

She amended it before she could stop herself. Then remembered that he could still hear.

A spasm of physical pain rippled across his face before he reached out a reluctant hand. The ruby glowed the second it touched his skin. He stared a split second, the slipped it into his pocket.

"You're going to be fine," he said firmly. "I'll be back with supplies before you know it."

She stared at him a second before remembering she was supposed to smile. It was hard to say whether it worked, but they came together a moment later in a weak but tender embrace.

"Just hold on, all right?" he whispered into her hair. "Will you do that for me?"

Her mind went deliberately blank as she nodded. "Yeah, I can do that."

His arms tightened a split second more before he pulled back. Like if he didn't let go that very moment, he'd go on holding her forever.

"All right." He moved quickly to the edge of the clearing, unable to look back for that final goodbye. "Keep close together until I return. No wandering off."

...like we have the strength to wander.

He kept talking, oblivious to the silence. To their sad, affectionate stares.

"Maybe stay in the cave," he continued. "I know what it looks like, but it will be the safest spot. In fact," he whipped around suddenly, "I can help you guys move—"

"Aidan," Cassiel interrupted with tired fondness, "...just go."

The world paused for a moment, then he gave them all one final stare, lingering an extra few seconds on a pair of twinkling eyes. Then he pulled in a quick breath, nodded, and vanished into the trees. Moving with such speed that the ground itself couldn't hold him, flying through the barren forest like there was a giant clock above him, counting down his family's final breaths.

Katerina and Cassiel stared at the spot he vanished from long after he was gone. Then they cast each other a quick look and settled down on the smooth stone.

All that was left to do was wait.

IT WAS HARD TO TELL whether she was awake or dreaming—that's one thing about dying that Katerina had never known.

As the hours dragged by she looked around countless times, only to realize that her eyes were already open. Other times she'd panic at the darkness, then realize they were already closed.

Tanya had never woken up since collapsing after the departure of the dragon, and Cassiel and Katerina didn't speak. It wasn't that they didn't want to. They simply didn't have the energy.

And what was there to say?

Time passed by at a crawl, dragging things out to the point where some secret part of them wished it would just hurry things along. Minutes stretched into hours. Hours stretched into years. A tiny breeze picked up mid-afternoon, providing some small semblance of relief, but it died down only an hour later. Leaving them breathless and burning on a ground baked with heat.

"Cass?"

His eyes opened slowly, staring at the grass, before lifting to her face. It had been a long time since either one of them had spoken. To be honest, she'd wondered if he was even going to reply.

"It might be cooler in the trees." She glanced at the shimmering forest halfway down the rocky hill. "Do you think we should try—"

"I can't move," he interrupted quietly.

He was lying flat on his back, ivory hair spilled over the desiccated leaves. Tanya's head was resting on his stomach, but she hadn't moved in quite some time. Neither had he. It had been long enough that he let out a little gasp as he tilted his head for a better view of the queen.

"Yeah," she answered softly. "Neither can I."

It hadn't been what she wanted to ask him. She knew what she wanted to ask him, but a part of her was terrified to hear his reply. A year ago, that would have stopped her. Now, she asked anyway.

"Do you think the Knight's going to kill him?"

She couldn't bring herself to say Dylan's name, any more than Cassiel could bring himself to hear it. He flinched at the mere implication before his beautiful face went very still.

For a moment, he didn't speak. Then he glanced at the knife in the mouth of the cave.

"I think he already did."

Not the wound—she knew he didn't mean the wound. It was serious and could easily kill him if left untreated, but the damage the Knight had done was more serious than that. While sparing the body, he had destroyed the mind. Eliminating free will. Erasing everything that had made the ranger himself. Whatever was left, if there was anything left, might not be enough to save.

Katerina turned her eyes elsewhere, gazing up at the sky. "Cass?"

"Hmm?"

"You would have been an amazing father."

He glanced at her in surprise, some indecipherable emotion shining on his face. Then all at once he looked impossibly, indescribably sad. Still, he managed to smile.

"...thank you."

It was quiet for a few minutes.

"What about me?" she finally asked. "Aren't you going to say I'd have made a great mom?"

His lips curved ever so slightly. "You want me to lie to you just because we're both about to die?"

She laughed weakly.

Even now. Even in the end.

"Cass—"

"Odds are, you would have misplaced the babe somewhere in the castle. Or forgotten you'd had one in the first place. It would be taken in by some kindly maid, raised on chestnuts and bark."

Katerina laughed again and rested her head on her arms. At first, she'd been too afraid to do so. Every time she'd put it down, she was afraid she wouldn't be able to lift it back up.

But those fears faded as the sun slipped closer towards the mountains.

Now, she wasn't afraid at all.

The conversation lapsed back into silence as each of the friends turned their minds to other things. One was absentmindedly stroking the hair of his beloved, the other was dreaming wistfully about hers. Wondering if he was still breathing. Wondering if he was wondering the same thing.

"You would have been a wonderful mother."

His voice caught her off guard and she glanced back, twisting her head on the ground.

"Yeah?"

Their eyes met with a soft smile.

"Your child would have been lucky to have you...and Dylan." His voice hitched ever so slightly as his eyes shone with quiet tears. "He would have forgiven you. You would have gotten back together."

They stared at each other for a moment longer before she bit her lip and had to look away.

"I'm sorry about the festival." She saw his questioning glance and clarified. "For coming to get you at the festival—all those months ago. If we hadn't, there's a chance you wouldn't have died."

How strange to be talking about it like it had already happened. How strange to be talking about it at all. And yet there was something strangely natural about it. Something almost calming about the inevitability. That they were in it together. There was no longer any fear.

"The festival," Cassiel murmured, remembering. Again, his lips curved in a gentle smile as he pressed a kiss to the top of Tanya's head. "You didn't kill me. You brought me back to life."

Those were the last words that were spoken. Even if the friends had wanted to keep the conversation going, they no longer had the breath to speak. Instead, they drifted into a deep but restless sleep—completely lost to everything happening in the world around them.

Katerina rolled onto her back, her pale face tilted towards the radiant sunset.

She didn't notice when her hair blew back off her forehead, when her dress fluttered in the sudden breeze. She didn't hear the beat of powerful wings as a dragon soared out of the sky...

Chapter 3

It smelled like wet dirt.

That was the first thing Katerina registered when her body reunited with her mind. The next was that she was slowly being smothered. The third was that some invisible person was crushing her hand. But it was the wet dirt that stuck with her.

She didn't understand it. To be wet, there had to be water. And if there was water, then she and her friends would have found it long ago. There was the possibility it had rained, though that didn't seem likely, which left her with nothing but the inexplicable smell.

Her eyes fluttered open, gazing up at the ceiling, before slowly focusing on the last person in the world she expected to see.

"...Kailas?"

There was a quiet gasp as her brother jumped in alarm. A second later, he hastened to drop her hand. A second after that, he picked it up again with a blush.

"Hi there." He leaned forward with a gentle smile, brushing back her hair. "You've been out for a while now. How are you feeling?"

She stared up at him in bewilderment, still half-convinced she was dreaming. Then her gaze floated over his shoulder to some potted violets, drops of water still clinging to their leaves.

"Did you water my plants?"

His face stilled in surprise before he glanced over his shoulder.

"Did I...?" He trailed off, not sure if she was joking. When she stared back in earnest, he struggled to gather his thoughts. "A maid came by, but I took the... Yeah, I watered them."

It was silent a moment, then he cocked his head with a little smile.

"Katy, I'm so glad you asked me—because this whole time you've been lying here I've been dying to talk about your plants."

Katerina blinked at him a moment, then smiled back. "...hi."

He laughed softly, leaning even closer as he squeezed her hand.

"You scared me." He gestured to the little camp he'd made in her room. "Scared me into stereotypes. I've been here by the bedside, fretting away."

It was said as a joke, but he meant it with all his heart. Judging by the dark hollows under his eyes, along with the plates of untouched food, he'd devoted himself entirely to the silent vigil.

"Watching me sleep, huh?" Katerina shifted higher on the pillows, secretly moved, but bound by the code of a big sister. "That's creepy."

He reached out quickly to help her, tucking the blanket around her waist.

"Haven't you heard? I'm the scourge of the five kingdoms." He kept his eyes down but flashed another quick smile. "*Creepy* isn't the half of it."

She wracked her brain, searching for a witty comeback, but fell utterly short. Her head was still spinning—trying desperately to come back to the present, to make sense of where she was.

"Are we..." She looked around, recognizing everything but coming up completely blank. "I don't understand... We're back in the castle?"

Kailas stared at her a moment, then nodded slowly. A second later he picked up a goblet of water, holding it carefully to her lips. When she shook her head, he simply waited. She finally drank.

"...that tastes incredible."

She tried to lift her hands to hold it herself, but was unable to move. Sometime in the night, someone had panicked and covered her with seven layers of suffocating blankets. Judging by her brother's slightly manic expression, she was beginning to suspect the culprit.

"Drink all of it," he warned softly, "or about a thousand people will have my head." When it got low enough, he lifted a pitcher and filled it back to the top. "That's it, nice and easy..."

She continued drinking for a moment, mostly just to stall and give her brain a little more time. Then she pulled her head away from the goblet and stared at her twin with wide eyes.

"Kailas, what happened?"

"Sera and I went to Vale, summoned the cavalry. We were already on our way back to the High Kingdom when we saw this...this *thing* swooping out of the sky." He shuddered in spite of himself, remembering the three-headed beast. "It only touched down for a few minutes before taking back off into the clouds. We thought...we thought maybe it came for you."

Without him saying another word, Katerina could easily imagine what happened next. The way her brother would strip off his cloak and turn into a dragon. The way Serafina would climb atop his back, and together the two of them would take to the skies.

He bowed his head suddenly, unable to look at her a second more.

"If I hadn't left—"

"If you hadn't left, you would have been trapped on that mountain just like all the rest of us," she interrupted quickly. Her brother had enough guilt in his life without adding more. "And there would have been no one left to rescue us and fly us home."

He nodded silently, knowing he'd still never forgive himself. She pulled in a faltering breath. A faint tremor shook through her hands as she cast him a tentative look.

"You didn't happen to see..." Another tremor rattled her fingers, and she clenched them in secret fists beneath the sheets. "Was there any sign of..."

Kailas shook his head. By now, he'd surely surmised that at least one of their number was missing. How much he knew beyond that was a mystery.

"The dragon?" she asked quickly, searching for any scrap of hope she could find. "Were you able to see where it—"

"By the time we got you back to the castle, the creature was gone."

However savage their world had become, at least her brother had the good manners not to show his relief. No matter how strong he was, any encounter with the beast would surely be his last.

There was a knock on the door.

Katerina looked over curiously, while her twin's shoulders wilted with a quiet sigh.

"You're not the only one who wants to talk about Dylan," he said quietly. "The Belarians aren't pleased." The door rattled and he sighed again. "I suppose you already know a man called—"

At that moment, the door kicked open and Atticus Gail flew inside. "She's awake?"

The words burst out of him as the twins stared back silently. Of course she was. She was looking right at him. But the man was so out of sorts, he could think of nothing else to say. Until—

"Where is he!"

A hint of disapproval flashed through Kailas' eyes as he tucked the blankets protectively around his sister. "She *just* woke up. After we found her *half-dead*. Give her a moment to—"

"No, it's all right." Katerina hitched herself higher on the bed, trying to pull herself together enough to recount the grisly tale. "Not long after the dwarf turned up dead in the forest, the seven of us were forced to dig him up on the off chance he was blind—"

Atticus held up a hand as Kailas squeezed her shoulder.

"I've told him all that. So has Sera. We showed up just a few hours after the spell had broken in the castle and, needless to say...there was a lot of explaining to do."

Yeah, I bet. Wait... the spell broke? Oh yeah, the wizard.

The last time Katerina had been inside the castle the ballroom was full of corpses, the stairwell had been pulled out of the floor, and three cave trolls were dead in the main foyer. She would guess there had been *quite* a lot of explaining. A part of her was happy she'd been asleep.

"We know everything that happened until the group of you separated in the forest." The head of the Belarian Council was breathless with anticipation, unravelling before her very eyes. "I have a vague idea of what happened next, but I...I need to hear it from you."

Katerina stared up at the man.

In all the time they'd known each other, she'd never seen him so uncertain. Not when Dylan had come back to Belaria to fight for his crown. Not even when he'd apologetically announced that his sovereign must end things with the woman he loved and marry another.

This time things were different. This time the man he'd sworn to protect wasn't hurt, or in exile, or in bed with a girl who wasn't his betrothed.

...he was simply gone.

"The Knight took him."

Even as Katerina said the words, she was almost unable to believe them herself. How could he just be gone? How could he have just vanished into the sky?

But it was far, *far* worse than that.

"The moment we killed the wizard, the cave filled with a blinding light. By the time we could see again, the Knight was standing there with..." She trailed off, still unable to say his name. "He said he didn't want it to be over, not just yet. He stabbed him with a cursed blade..."

...and my entire world fell apart.

Atticus made a strange motion with his head, almost as if he was both nodding and shaking it at the same time. His fingers were trembling and his skin had gone a sickly shade of grey.

"That's what Cassiel said," he murmured. "A *doronos*. But I can't believe..."

A moment later he started pacing, muttering under his breath as if the royal twins weren't even there. Katerina stared after him a moment before suddenly lifting her head.

Cassiel. Tanya.

She'd been so disoriented since waking, she hadn't thought to ask about her other friends.

"Are they all right?" She turned to her brother, still standing protectively over her as the councilman muttered and paced. "Cass and Tanya. And you and Sera...you're all right?"

He glanced back down at her before giving a swift nod.

"Everyone's alive. The three of you were on your way out...but everyone's alive."

The three of us...

It was coming back to her more quickly now, the longer she stayed awake. Without a word of warning she grabbed the goblet once again, draining it in five giant gulps. Now was no time to be shaky. There were important things to discuss.

"That's great, Katy." Her twin knelt down with an encouraging smile, picking up a platter of fruit that had been left on the side of the bed. "Do you think you could try some of this—"

"What about Aidan?"

In hindsight, she didn't know why she was asking. Her brother had left long before anything had happened, and the vampire himself was the cause. Even as she said the name, a dark emotion flitted across the prince's face. He cleared it with a tight smile, glancing at the door.

"How do you think we found you?"

For the second time the door burst open, the vampire flying inside. There was no way to track him. He was nothing more than a blur of shadow, rematerializing beside the bed.

"Kat." He knelt beside her, looking like a man who had come back to life. In a matter of seconds his body relaxed, his hands steadied, and a spark of light settled in his eyes. "How are you feeling?"

He didn't need to touch her skin to get a pulse but he did it anyway, wrapping his long fingers around her wrist, needing to feel it for himself.

She tried to roll her eyes, but found herself too tired. "I'm fine. You can call off the eulogy."

Neither the prince nor the vampire saw the humor. For that matter neither the prince nor the vampire were looking at each other, even though they were standing only a few feet away.

"How long have I been out?"

She sat up suddenly on the bed, surprised she hadn't asked sooner. Atticus was still talking to himself, but the others reached down at the same time to steady her.

Kailas' face went rigid. Aidan slowly retracted his hand.

"Two days," Kailas said softly. "Tanya still hasn't woken up, but her grandmother's with her now and says things look good. She also..." He trailed off abruptly, going red. "She's very friendly."

Katerina flashed a wicked grin as Aidan pursed his lips to hide a smile.

Both remembered the first time that they'd wandered into the jungle hut and met the Kreo chief. At the time, the old woman had been quite taken with Tanya's own boyfriend. One of the first things she did after guaranteeing them safe passage was demand that he take off his pants.

Katerina was about to ask about it, her sluggish mind taking a second to click on, but then her twin's voice rang again through her mind.

Two days.

"Dylan," she whispered.

For two days he had been in that man's evil clutches. For two days he'd been in a land of darkness, facing those monsters and demons all on his own.

...while I slept.

"Yes. *Dylan.*"

Atticus circled suddenly back to them, finding it harder and harder to rein in his temper. A part of him knew it wasn't their fault. A part of him (like the rest of the newly awoken councils) was simply astounded that the young royals had managed to stay alive so long on their own.

But it was *his* king who was missing. All the others had returned.

"While I am exceedingly relieved the rest of you made it back in one piece, Your Majesty, I really must insist that we gather in the High Chamber to discuss what's going to be done."

Katerina's eyes softened as they rested on his face.

In her kingdom, there was no High Chamber—that was a Belarian institution. Hers had only a Great Hall. The man knew this, but things were starting to slip through the panic.

"Yes, of course," she said softly, pushing to her feet. "We'll assemble at once."

"No."

A single, quiet command. But it stopped every other voice in the room.

By the time the queen registered her twin had released her, the warmth had yet to fade from her hand. She looked down at it, then looked up at him—arms folded, standing in front of her bed.

"She just opened her eyes and you want her to attend some meeting?"

For a split second, Katerina remembered why everyone in the five kingdoms had found her twin brother so terrifying. For a split second, she was willing to bet Atticus Gail remembered, too.

But while he had the sense to hold his tongue, she tugged tentatively on her brother's sleeve.

"Kailas, this isn't—"

He caught her hand without looking, squeezing it gently.

"—it isn't up for discussion." Those dark eyes burned like embers as he glared the Belarian Councilman down. "My sister almost *died* up on that mountain. She needs to rest. And if you think that's not what Dylan himself would have commanded, then you don't know the man you serve."

Would have commanded...

Whatever half-hearted defense Atticus attempted, the queen never heard it. She was stuck on her brother's wording. *Would have.* As in, Dylan would have commanded it if he were here? Or did her brother mean Dylan would have commanded it if he was still able to be making such orders.

A chill ran up the backs of her knees, settling somewhere in her chest.

"Kailas," she said softly, ignoring Aidan's cautioning hand as she pushed to her feet, "I want to do this. I-I need to. Dylan would do it for me."

...would have done it for me?

Aidan's eyes flashed up, but he said nothing. Instead he turned, like Atticus, to her brother. Waiting for him to decide. Kailas held her gaze for a long moment, then let out a quiet sigh.

"You sound like Cassiel."

Even as he spoke, an explosion of sound echoed from the other end of the corridor. An unholy series of shouts and violent impacts, all silenced by a truly breathtaking curse.

The friends stared at the door, momentarily going still.

"Cass will have a harder time," Aidan murmured.

Before Katerina could ask what he meant, there was another explosion from much closer this time. Just a moment later, the door burst open yet again. This time, there was no salvaging it.

It hung crooked on the hinges, with a beautiful fae standing in the frame.

Like the queen, Cassiel seemed to have spent the last few days lying in bed. And like the queen, he seemed to have awoken to an anxious entourage. No sooner had he appeared at the door than at least ten more fae raced up behind him. One of them was nursing a black eye and clutching his chest at the speed of the chase. Another was still holding a cup of ice chips.

"Good. You're awake."

Katerina could have been recently fished from an active volcano and probably still would have gotten the same response. One that hovered between indifference and impatience. Any and all affection was hidden meticulously underneath.

She raised her head with the ghost of a grin. "Nice clothes."

The normally impeccably-dressed woodland prince was wearing a rather odd ensemble. A white tunic unlaced almost all the way to the navel, and black breeches she was fairly certain had been put on the wrong way. His silken hair was hanging in loose waves around his face, and while he may have remembered to grab his sword his shoes remained on the other side of the castle.

It was as if he'd started to get dressed, then decided he'd rather go on a rampage instead.

"Nice face," he answered without missing a beat, smirking as she lifted two hands to her cheeks. "We have to go. They've called a meeting in the Grand Pavilion."

She stared at him a moment, tilting her head.

For the second time, one of the great lords had gotten it wrong. The High Kingdom didn't have a Grand Pavilion—that was a relic of Taviel. But the High-Born prince was too distracted to notice. Indeed, he had yet to notice that he wasn't wearing any shoes.

"Get *up*, Katerina. What are you waiting for?"

There was a disapproving sound as the man with the ice chips shook his head, muttering the Fae word for *manners*. Cassiel ignored him, those dark eyes were locked on Katerina.

"What's the problem?"

She shifted anxiously on her feet, glancing at the back of her brother's head.

"No problem...I'm coming now."

The last thing she needed was more trouble between the two men. It was bad enough that the last time the two had spoken, her brother had lost his temper entirely and shouted in the fae's face. There was a strong argument to be made for the fact that Cassiel had it coming. But, given the precariousness of their current situation, she didn't want to push that now.

"Are you sure you're up for this?" Kailas asked quietly, bracing her weight as she hobbled towards the closet. "I could go in your place. Say whatever you want. Tell you what happens—"

"You're too well-spoken," Cassiel cut him off shortly. "They'd never believe it was actually Katerina doing the talking. Besides, who would trip in the entryway if we left her behind?"

The Damaris twins stopped in their tracks, sharing a quick look.

Did that just...? Did he really...?

Did Cassiel just give Kailas a compliment?

"There's also a good chance someone will try to shoot you again if you step inside that room," the fae continued conversationally. "There's an even better chance that person will be me."

...there it is.

Chapter 4

Considering how many strange things had happened in the castle over the last few years, it was still a rather odd processional to be marching down the halls.

Cassiel was in the front, eyes dilated and hair blowing out behind him, sweeping barefoot across the marble floor. The entourage of fae was just a step or two behind—trying to keep up with their prince's unforgiving pace while attempting to finish dressing him at the same time. Aidan followed along after. His first instinct had been to help Katerina, but one look at her twin brother's face had successfully rid him of that notion. Instead, he was positioned as a sort of bridge between the two groups, walking side by side with Atticus Gail. That just left the Damaris twins.

One of whom was having a hard time.

"Just let me carry you," Kailas murmured for the fifth time. "If you insist upon this ridiculous notion, at least let me make sure you don't fall down along the way."

His hand shot out to steady her as she slipped on the slick floor.

"It isn't ridiculous," Katerina said through gritted teeth, trying to find her balance. "*You're* ridiculous," she added for good measure.

He shot her a memorable look, but said nothing.

Truth be told, he was a lot more worried about his sister than he was letting on. Especially considering he'd spent the last two days counting her breaths and feeding her ice chips. But since their unlikely reunion in the castle dungeon, he'd come to realize certain things had changed. Gone was the thoughtful, soft-spoken girl who'd cringed when he came around a corner, and spent hours in the castle garden, dreaming of adventures that would never come. She'd been replaced by a queen with a certain degree of reckless disregard for things like common sense and personal safety.

And if that queen was insisting upon rounding up the leaders of the five kingdoms whilst suffering from borderline delirium, there was nothing he or anyone else could do to stop it.

That being said...his sister was secretly grateful for the supportive hand.

Where are you? What is he doing to you?

She'd dressed in a simple gown. She'd made conversation and smiled when others had tried to make conversation back. She'd acted like she was paying attention.

Like she wasn't still in that cave. Like she wasn't screaming inside her head.

Do you know who you are? Do you know that I love you?

Everything had gone fuzzy after that three-headed dragon had swooped out of the clouds, nearly decapitating the lot of them and carrying the man she loved into a stormy sky. She barely remembered talking with Cassiel. She barely remembered the feel of the parched earth beneath her brow. But two things remained perfect in her memory. A question and an answer. Each one pulled from the very depths of a broken heart. Each one more devastating than that last.

Do you think the Knight's going to kill him?

She'd asked Cassiel in a moment of dark honesty, a moment when they both thought they were going to die. He had no reason to lie to her. There'd been nothing but genuine pain in his eyes.

I think he already did.

And just like that, she'd started to unravel. Because of all the ways she'd tried to prepare herself, all the things she'd braced for over the last few months...this was not one of them.

She'd expected death. She'd expected torture. She'd expected a narrow win, or a devastating loss. The pendulum swung one way or another. There was no middle ground in between.

But this? This was nothing *but* middle ground.

The ranger was gone, yet his body remained. He still drew breath, yet there wasn't a trace of him left in those blue eyes. It was a forced purgatory. One that left Katerina faced with something she couldn't have possibly imagined. A world in which the two of them weren't on the same side.

...are you even alive?

"Katerina."

She jerked out of her trance, staring into her brother's eyes. His handsome face was tight with concern. The giant doors to the Great Hall lay just a few steps ahead.

"We're here," he said softly, wishing very much it wasn't the case. He cast a quick look behind them before lowering his voice. "Are you *sure* about this? The people in there can wait."

A din of voices drifted past the doors, many more voices than she'd been expecting when she'd left her bedroom just a few minutes before. Cassiel paused as well, tensing nervously before reaching down to lace up his tunic. A second later, their eyes met with a quick nod.

"But Dylan can't."

Without another word, they kicked open the heavy doors.

Every conversation stopped. Every head turned. A *lot* of heads. Katerina had assumed only the leaders of the various councils would be present, but by the look of things almost every member of every visiting delegation had packed themselves inside. It was standing room only, with over a hundred people craning to get a glimpse as the young royals tentatively stepped inside.

Never had she seen such open amazement. Such gawking faces from those trained by years of protocol to keep those sorts of emotions at bay. None of them could summon a coherent thought or find a word to speak. None of them could lift their hands in applause or bow their heads in respect. They only stood there, staring just as helplessly as she and her friends were staring back.

Because, in their minds...only a few days have passed.

For the first time since learning the spell over the castle had lifted, Katerina understood the strange disparity in terms of their shared sense of time. As far as the people inside were concerned, they'd seen the monarchs only a few hours before. They were still reeling from the assassination attempt, from the dwarf and the fae who had died just a few hours after. Events that seemed like another lifetime ago to the recently returned travelers, still hovering uncertainly in the doorway.

They had no knowledge of anything that had happened since. Of the demons, or the ghouls, or the mermaids, or the trolls. Of the Carpathian horde, or the cannibalistic villagers, or the wicked darkness spreading like poison over the land. If it wasn't for the rotting bodies still being discreetly funneled out of the dungeon, for the stains of blood still covering the walls, they would have no way to know that they'd been frozen statues amidst a grisly battle. That they'd stood, lifeless and serene, while a handful of teenagers fought desperately in the halls around them, drenched in royal blood.

She couldn't imagine the shock when the spell had suddenly lifted and they blinked open their heretofore enchanted eyes. She couldn't imagine the terror when they found the Kasi swarm in the ballroom, the body of a mythical Carpathian lion lying on the dungeon floor.

It must have been quiet. Very quiet. Until they started to scream.

Then the frenzy would have begun.

Bodies would be counted and recounted, chambers would be searched. Each layer of blood would add another layer of panic as the kingdoms tallied their numbers. As they swarmed every inch of the blood-soaked castle, searching for those who were missing, grieving for those who were lost.

Only to discover their young heroes were nowhere to be found.

But Petra was here. The queen spotted the strange woman standing in the corner. Her brother Michael was by her side. *Petra would have told them what happened.*

"It was bad," Kailas said softly as people started pushing towards them and conversations broke out anew. "Some of them were collateral in the battle. Some of them never woke up."

Katerina let out a quiet sigh. As hard as they'd tried to keep their frozen subjects out of harm's way, the creatures they were fighting had no such qualms. She remembered a cloaked changeling using a pair of Belarian infantrymen as a shield. Five more had vanished without a sound as part of the ceiling collapsed in the East Wing. Surely many others had been lost amidst the bloody fray.

"I'm assuming we don't need to summarize?" she asked quickly under her breath. Already, she could see the head of her own council, Abel Bishop, fighting towards her through the crowd. A man so robotic and critical, she couldn't imagine recounting the outlandish events of the last few weeks. "You and Sera have already told them what happened?"

Her brother nodded, following the man's progress as well.

"That was two days of intense interrogation I wouldn't care to repeat."

The prince was tightly wound, but his dark eyes softened as they swept over the room.

"Not that you can really blame them," he continued quietly. "They woke up in a demolished castle, covered in blood, then looked outside to see a giant dragon landing on the roof. Dylan was gone, Sera and Aidan were wrecks, and the three of you were pale as corpses."

He glanced again at the swarming masses, shifting uncomfortably in his skin.

"Most of them probably thought I was just dropping off the bodies..."

At first, Katerina didn't understand. Then all at once, it clicked.

For what had felt like an eternity she and her twin brother had been flying around the five kingdoms, fighting for their lives. They'd crossed from one side of the realm to the other, facing unspeakable terrors, sacrificing every last bit of themselves in that endless quest for the greater good.

It had been a fantastical journey, filled with more heartbreak than most people would see in a lifetime. But amidst all the bad, she'd received something just as impossibly good.

...she'd gotten her brother back.

Kailas was no longer seen as a threat. He'd become an invaluable asset. Spilling blood beside them, fighting as one of them. She couldn't count the number of times the friends had leaned on that quiet pragmatism, the quick flash of his sword. The sins of the past had been swept away to reveal the man beneath. She would trust that man with anything. She'd trust him with her life.

But not everyone felt the same.

The last time Kailas had been in the Great Hall, some unknown assassin had tried to take his life. The identity of the killer had been impossible to determine, because there wasn't a man, woman, or child in the five kingdoms who didn't want to see him hanged from the nearest tree. Most of the people flooding towards them now had personally demanded his life. Some of them very recently. It would take more than a few impossible acts of heroism to change their minds.

...or so she thought.

"What a blessed morning, Your Highness!" Abel Bishop reached them at last, clasping his hands together in an unprecedented display of emotion. "You must be so relieved!"

Katerina froze in surprise as Kailas lifted his head slowly, shocked to see the councilman's warm greeting was directed at him. It took a moment to gather his senses. A moment that might have lasted much longer if his sister hadn't discreetly nudged him in the back.

"Uh...yes, thank you. I'm very relieved."

Bishop smiled at him before bowing low to his sister. "Your Majesty." The words caught in his throat as he fought the urge to gather the young woman protectively in his arms. "I cannot begin to...I'm so *pleased* you've made it back unharmed."

Her eyebrows lifted in surprise. Considering the man's famously stoic sensibilities, that was practically a song and dance. She shared a quick look with Kailas, then motioned for him to rise.

"Thank you, Abel," she answered sweetly, feeling rather touched. "It wasn't for lack of trying, I can tell you that. And it wasn't anything I could have done by myself."

"Yes," he said fervently, "I've been told."

Without another word he strode across the tile, interrupting Cassiel in the middle of a hushed conversation and extending his hand. "You have my eternal thanks, my lord."

The fae looked up in surprise then shook the proffered hand slowly, his dark eyes flickering over the man's shoulder to where the queen and her brother were watching side by side.

"I did nothing they haven't done for me a thousand times over," he said graciously. "The debt of gratitude is my own."

A polite deflection, but the councilman wasn't fooled. Instead of releasing the fae he tightened his grip, pulling him closer with a little smile.

"That's very kind, but you saved both my prince and my queen." His voice rose protectively with each one. "The fae are a strong people, with a history of taking care of themselves. But know that if you ever have need of it, the High Kingdom will ride to your aid."

This time, Cassiel didn't know what to say. They had deviated from the script entirely, and he could do nothing but stare as Bishop turned his attention elsewhere.

"And you, Ambassador...there is nothing we can ever do to repay you."

Aidan tensed in surprise, but said nothing. The rest of the Hall had fallen silent to watch as the leaders of the land converged. Over a hundred pairs of eyes were trained on their every move.

"We have not yet received your brethren," Bishop continued cordially. "But rest assured, they will be offered every possible accommodation the moment they arrive."

Katerina's eyes snapped up as Kailas stiffened. Apparently, he and Sera hadn't told the councils everything. Maybe they were feeling protective. Maybe they thought it wasn't their place.

Maybe they were both a little more scared of Merrick than they had let on.

Aidan's face paled, but he forced a polite smile. "Thank you."

There will be time enough to get to that later. At the moment, we have more crucial matters to discuss.

The queen was impatient, but the acknowledgements and commendations were just getting started. Once the story about the young royals had begun to circulate, it seemed that everyone had something to say. Everyone had someone to thank.

And those people rarely belonged to the same kingdom.

Men were making covenants with witches. Fae were shaking hands with dwarves. It seemed that the five kingdoms didn't need banquets or eloquent speeches to bring them together. They needed only a common goal. To protect and defend the circle of people standing in front of them.

And for the first time, that circle included someone new.

"Your Highness."

Kailas whirled around in surprise to see a group of Kreo warlocks standing before him, the same warlocks that had stood in the same hall just weeks before and demanded his head. He tensed automatically, looking them up and down, but they simultaneously sank into a bow.

"After we heard about everything you..." The man speaking for them trailed off, looking a little overwhelmed. "Needless to say you have our sincerest apologies, my lord. No one should know better than us the potency of a sorcerer's spell. We were wrong to judge. We're so very sorry."

The handsome prince froze with the expression of someone who'd had more than his share of death threats in the last few years. But the warlocks were just the tip of the iceberg.

One by one, the aristocracy of the five kingdoms stepped forward to offer their sincerest apologies and their most heartfelt thanks. Each one peeling off another layer of guilt. Each one acting as another stepping-stone in that endless road of redemption.

By the time they were finished, Kailas looked as though he needed to lie down. His skin was flushed but his eyes were bright, shining every so often with what might have been a secret tear.

Katerina stood silently beside him. Crying when he could not. Beaming with unspeakable pride. But it wasn't long before her eyes flickered over his shoulder to the edge of the crowd.

There was one kingdom that hadn't joined in the celebration. A group of shifters that stood motionless on the sidelines without saying a word.

Michael was amongst them.

"So it's true," he said grimly, his quiet voice cutting over the crowd. "Dylan is gone."

Katerina's breath caught in her chest. Since that fateful moment in the cave, it seemed as though everyone was incapable of saying the ranger's name. She most of all. But of course, Michael had no such problems. He swept gracefully through the crowd, appearing by her side.

"He was taken," she answered in a faltering voice. "He's not...gone."

However, to be honest, she didn't know if there was a difference. Up until a few days ago, she'd thought that a *doronos* was a blade of myth. She had no idea if its effects were reversible, and she'd been hoping the immortal shifter would cue her in.

From the moment they met in the halls of Talsing Sanctuary so long ago, she'd secretly believed the man could do anything. It was a faith that had come long before he'd sprouted angelic wings and leapt off the mountain's peak. As if her instincts weren't enough, Dylan's own confidence in the man had been catching. The ranger was the strongest man she knew, independent to a fault, but he trusted in Michael completely. His plans would change at the man's slightest suggestion. Well-established hopes and fears shifted at a single distracted word.

But for the first time, she found no comfort in that familiar face.

In the bright lights of the room, his face was clouded in shadow. Oblivious to the hordes of people staring at him for guidance. Staring into the distance, seeing only a single face.

Petra put a hand on her brother's shoulder.

"There is an old castle in the heart of the badlands. Made from glass and dark stone. It would be nothing but a ruin now, but if the boy is alive that's where he would be."

"The Castle of Sorne?" Henry Chambers interjected with a shudder. "That's real?"

There was a hushed murmur behind him, but it extinguished quickly.

"I've seen it," Petra said shortly. "It's as real as you or me."

"Then we should destroy it." A gruff voice spoke up from the back of the crowd as a stout dwarf stepped forward. "If there's any sort of castle, that's likely where we'll find the Red Knight."

Under most circumstances, he would fall under the Kreo umbrella—to be represented as such. But both Tanya and her grandmother were conspicuously missing from the Great Hall.

"Destroy it?" Cassiel interrupted sharply. "Did you not hear what Petra just said? If Dylan is alive, he is most likely in the castle."

"He's been stabbed by a *doronos* blade."

It was impossible to tell who'd spoken—the voice came from someone in the middle of the crowd. But several people were already nodding along, a hard determination in their eyes.

"We need to take the castle as quickly as possible," one of the witches urged. "If the army that Fell assembled is as impressive as they say—"

"We will do *nothing* until we get Dylan back," Cassiel interrupted again, even sharper than before. "As far as this conclave is concerned, that is our *only* priority."

There was a murmur throughout the crowd, though no one seemed willing to challenge him directly. Even the other fae were staring at each other uncertainly before glancing at their prince.

Only the shifters were silent. Katerina got the feeling their minds were made up either way.

"Our only hope of defeating the Knight is the prophecy," Aidan reasoned softly. "It speaks of *five* people to stand through the flood. There's no point in going forward if we don't—"

"The prophecy was broken before—it is broken again." A general from Katerina's own army cast her an apologetic look, but held his ground. "Your friend is lost, Your Majesty. I'm sorry to say it, but it's true. There's no point in hinging our hopes on some ancient guesswork based around the unification of five people, when there are only four. We must attack now. We must fight."

There was a blur of white hair, then Cassiel was standing in front of him.

"Say that again."

In a flash, the room erupted in noise. As quickly as the five kingdoms had united, they were divided once again. Each person shouting their own opinion. Violently waving hands in the air as they shouted and made threats, and effectively unraveled every shred of alliance they'd worked to build.

Katerina watched without speaking, rooted to the spot.

There was a ringing in her ears, a tingling in her palms and, try as she might, she couldn't understand what they were saying. She couldn't understand how they were so quick to give up and formulate a new strategy. She couldn't understand how they could discount the shifters and abandon the prophecy. She couldn't understand how they were talking about Dylan like he was already dead.

Cassiel and Atticus were shouting, standing side by side. Leonor looked worried and Michael was rubbing his eyes, while Petra stared at him with great concern.

One by one, things were falling apart. One by one, people were staring to break.

But to Katerina, things had never been more clear.

"We go to war," she said quietly.

The room feel silent as a hundred eyes turned her way. She didn't need to see them, she could feel them instead. Each one burning into her as her eyes lifted to a single patch of sky.

"To save the five kingdoms...and to bring Dylan back alive."

Chapter 5

What originally started as a peace summit ended as a declaration of war.

It helped that it had always been on the distant horizon. It helped that the people of the realm had always known the Red Knight would need to be stopped. Since before the delegations had even arrived, their respective kingdoms had already begun stockpiling supplies. Soldiers whose years of active duty had passed were called back into service. Those already enlisted were thrown into a fierce daily regimen of training and drills. Weapons were sharpened and polished. Strong metals from deep in the earth were melted down to make more. Horses were saddled. Armor was packed.

By the time the friends left the High Kingdom, they did so with no less than seven battalions from every part of the realm.

Katerina and Kailas led the way at the head of the Royal Army. The silver banners of the Fae were riding at their side. Henry Chambers and the cavalrymen from the Vale brought up the left wing, while the Kreo forces held down the right. Petra's rebels made up the bulk of the center, along with the Talsing warriors who'd answered Michael's call.

It was an impressive display. But perhaps none so much as the army from Belaria. For they had decided to make the journey not as men...but as wolves.

Katerina glanced over her shoulder, riding tall on her childhood steed.

Even though she knew they were on the same side, the sight of the fearsome pack stalking forward was still enough to give her chills. Many of the horses had spooked the second they left the castle. Some of them had to wear blinders so they couldn't see anything behind.

She could see Atticus prowling near the front. Before each of his adolescent escapes to his girlfriend's castle, Dylan had been very clear that the head of the council had full power to act in his stead. It wasn't in the man's nature to fight; diplomacy ran strong in his blood.

But wolves were different. And ever since hearing the king to whom he'd pledged his life had been taken, a light had gone out in the councilman's eyes. A dark momentum governed him now, driving him forward ceaselessly. He moved like a ghost, carrying something in his mouth.

It took Katerina a second to realize it was Dylan's sword.

Ronin the mercenary was walking close beside him, shaggy black fur and glistening teeth, a band of roguish wolves trailing behind him. They must have only just made it to Belaria before they'd been made to turn around. Upon waking, Katerina had been told by a chambermaid that when her brother wasn't fretting by her bedside, he'd been up in the sky—ferrying people to the castle from every corner of the High Kingdom. It was a miracle he could stay on his horse.

"Are you okay?" she asked softly, shooting him a side glance.

He blinked quickly then nodded, making a visible effort to keep himself awake. "I'm fine. What about you?"

She smiled weakly, turning back to the bleak horizon. "Fine."

Brave words, but she didn't know how anything could be fine in a place like this. She'd never seen anything like it. Nothing but parched, barren earth as far as the eye could see.

"This used to be underwater," Cassiel said quietly, nudging his horse to the queen's side. "I remember hearing about it as a boy. They called it the Roan Sea."

The twins looked over in amazement, unable to imagine it, then turned as he pointed into the distance. Sure enough, if you strained your eyes you could still see the distant crest of waves on the horizon. But they seemed to be getting farther away the longer they looked.

"How is that possible?" Katerina mused, staring at the desiccated ground.

It was cracked and splintered, littered with the carcasses of dead fish and other larger creatures. Several of which looked vaguely human, except for the long tails.

It must have happened so quickly. But how could...?

She lifted her eyes to the horizon, then decided it was one answer she didn't want to know.

FOR THE NEXT SEVEN hours the vast army marched across the wasteland, moving at a slower and slower pace. A kind of haze had fallen over the sky, and waves of heat rose off the land in shimmering spirals. As time progressed, several of the foot soldiers fell to their knees and had to be carried. Not long after that, the rest of them dismounted in an effort to spare the horses.

Sweat was dripping down faces. The wolves were panting and pawing at the ground. One by one, people started taking off pieces of armor. A helmet here. A cloak there. Even Abel Bishop, a man who'd never once sacrificed his composure, handed off his sword so he could remove his cape and the thick layer of chainmail underneath.

At first, Katerina worried it was some kind of strategy—like the wizard who'd surrounded himself with three days of starvation from every side. A dastardly trick to leave them weak and unprotected—not wearing their armor, but carrying it instead.

But the ground was perfectly flat in every direction. If anyone was headed towards them, they'd be able to see it coming from miles away. The greater problem by far was that the enemy didn't seem to care that they were coming. The endless desert was nothing but a geographical bonus. They'd see who made it to the other side. Until then, they were perfectly content to wait.

"Kat, watch out!"

The queen looked down just in time to see the little scorpion skittering towards her. At the exact same moment Aidan's arm circled around her waist, lifting her out of the way. He crushed it a second later under his heel, grinding it for good measure into the withered ground.

"What is it?" Cassiel swept towards them in alarm. "What's wrong?"

Aidan squinted his eyes against the sun, scanning around for more. "Scorpion."

There was a muffled shout from the ranks behind them as a tall soldier still wearing his helmet slipped to the ground. Another was soon to follow. And another after that. In addition to the paralyzing heat, they'd apparently stumbled into some kind of nest.

"Just keep moving!" Cassiel raised his voice to be heard, pointing a few steps ahead of them to where a hand-sized spider was digging itself out of the ground. Kailas stared a moment in disgust, then fired out a ribbon of flame. "They die easily enough. Keep an even pace, stay in formation."

With exaggerated caution the army proceeded forward, moving slowly and scanning the ground before every step. A sting from a scorpion would be bad enough, but things had an extra bite in the Dunes. With a shudder, Katerina remembered the Hypache viper in the Carpathian pit. It had come from here. Just like the basilisk. And her brother's hounds. Every nightmarish creature in the world seemed to have crawled out of this one hellish place.

Should just blast the whole thing off the face of the earth, she thought sullenly, lifting the skirt of her dress so she could see her feet. *Douse it in fire—*

A sudden noise interrupted her thoughts, as wild as it was unexpected. The friends turned around at the same time then froze where they stood, lips parted in surprise.

"Are they laughing?" Kailas asked incredulously.

Cassiel opened his mouth to answer, then simply nodded with a smile.

In a twist of events none of them could have predicted the combination of heat, exhaustion, and scorpions proved to be too much. Hoots of tired, uncontrollable laughter rang from one end of the procession to the other as scores of witches perched like snipers on the horses, firing down balls of green and yellow light. The fae were too dignified to participate, even though Katerina could see several of them itching to reach for their bows, but the wolves were the real stars of the show.

They were yipping, and pouncing, and rolling on their backs like puppies—rooting around in the sand to drive the deadly little creatures from their holes. In a game as lively as it was dangerous some of them were tossing the scorpions back and forth, seeing how long they could keep them up in the air, before one of them would lose control and rip it to pieces in their teeth. There were a few cries of genuine pain as drops of scorching venom sizzled their fur, but wolves played hard.

"Pack of mutts," Cassiel scoffed, but he said it with a grin. "You can see now why they crowned *Dylan* as king—"

He cut himself off suddenly, stricken to have said the name. A wave of emotion swept over his face as he stared at the playful wolves. Then he leapt onto his horse and rode out in front of the army, keeping his eyes locked on the grey nothingness up ahead.

Katerina stared at the back of his head.

She'd been doing her best to keep it together. Even when her head was swimming with dark images and endless questions. Even when her heart was literally aching for him with every step. But, for whatever reason, seeing Cassiel's broken reaction was the final step.

As she continued marching into the desert, she began to cry.

There was an awkward moment behind her, one she would never see. Both Kailas and Aidan had taken an automatic step forward, then glanced at each other and froze. A muscle twitched in the prince's jaw, but he softened as he thought of his sister. After a few strained seconds, he tilted his head in her direction—a silent invitation for the vampire to go ahead.

Aidan appeared beside her a moment later. Saying nothing. It was enough to be close. They continued walking for a bit, tuning out the noise behind them, before she forced herself to speak.

"...can you sense him?"

It was the question she'd been waiting to ask ever since she woke up to find herself back at the castle. The second the words were out of her mouth, she realized she'd been saving them. There was too much at stake. She was too afraid to say them out loud.

Aidan and Dylan had bonded. An eternal blood bond. If one of them was no longer able to sense the other...then hope was truly lost.

"Just say it quickly," she blurted before he could answer, balling her hands and clenching her teeth. "I can't take it—"

"I can't sense him," Aidan answered carefully. "...but I don't think he's dead."

She stopped in her tracks, turning to him with tear-stained cheeks. "What does that mean?"

His eyes softened with unspeakable pity, fastening on her trembling face. "I'd know if he'd been killed," he said softly. "I'd be able to feel it. I've...I've been *waiting* to feel it. But I haven't. He might be lost to me...but he's alive."

A small flicker of hope stirred inside her, too small to even see.

"You really mean that?" she whispered, studying his face for any hint of a lie. "You're not just saying it? You really think he's alive?"

"Yes, I do." He raised his voice slightly, just loud enough for the fae to hear. "And as long as he draws breath, there's a chance to undo what's been done. I don't know how, but if anyone can come back from something like this...it's Dylan."

Cassiel's breathing hitched, though he never turned around. He continued riding as if he hadn't heard a thing. Katerina wasn't quite so contained. Without thinking she leapt on top of the vampire, wrapping her arms around his neck in a tight embrace.

"Thank you," she whispered. "Thank you for saying that."

His arms tightened, holding her effortlessly in the air. "I'm not just saying it, Kat. He really is—"

"I know," she interrupted, burying her face in the collar of his shirt. "Just...thank you."

In the mother of all ironies, things had been significantly easier with Aidan since their forbidden kiss in the woods. There was no longer any mystery. None of those burning questions they couldn't answer by themselves. If it weren't for the fact that it had ripped her relationship with the ranger to shreds, she might have actually been grateful for it. The second their lips touched, it was like turning back the hands of time. Now they could return to the way things were.

That flicker of hope made her almost giddy, and with a sudden giggle she kicked him in the shins. "Put me down, monster. Haven't you learned not to touch me by now?"

He stared down at her, lips parting in surprise. "...we're joking about that?"

He's alive. Aidan can feel it. He might not be himself...but he's alive.

"What else can we do?" She kicked him again then dropped to the ground, ignoring the sharp sting that laced up the side of her ankle. The wolves were still frolicking behind her, and for the first time since they'd started the sight of it made her smile. "Better to laugh about it, right?"

He's alive. And as long as that's true—there's a chance for us.

She was breathing too quickly and her head was practically spinning with delight. Already, the burnt colors of the desert had started to blur.

"You're right, Aidan. We're going to get him back."

Without a backward glance, she took off marching towards the horizon. Oblivious to the fact that the vampire was watching her strangely. Oblivious to her torn shoe.

"We're going to get him back...then everything will go back to normal."

Chapter 6

Katerina didn't know how many more hours passed before a Belarian general finally suggested that they make camp. At first, the endless marching had seemed like a badge of honor, an unofficial competition between the different factions of the group. Then, once the scorching skies got even a bit cooler, everyone wanted to capitalize on the temperature and get as far as they could.

The place they finally stopped was as strange as the place from which they'd just come. A little oasis right in the middle of the desert heat. It was clearly not the first time it had been used for such a purpose. It was rare that traders and merchants would venture all the way to the Dunes, but if ever they did it was the precise spot where all of them had made camp.

Traces of it were still visible. Charred stones from the base of a fire. A conical indent in the packed ground where someone had attempted a failed well. One of the traders lived in Vale and had actually come with them to act as a guide. He was talking to several heads of council, pointing to random grooves in the distance that might have been roads, speaking a dialect she didn't understand.

They would get better directions from Michael and Petra once they got closer, but the rough terrain was always changing—and the siblings had nothing yet to offer. Truth be told, Michael hadn't said a word since learning Dylan had been taken. He simply stared into the distance, riding a slate grey horse, oblivious to the army around him. A quiet storm brewing in those immortal eyes.

When was the last time he was here? The final day of the First War? Had he stopped at this same camp, travelled along these same roads...preparing to battle one of his best friends?

Katerina watched him quietly, then followed his gaze with a shiver.

The place was a nightmare. And Dylan was there all alone.

With a quiet sigh she settled down on the grass beside the rest of them, heart racing, feeling feverish and weak. Normally, the traveling army would be pitching the white infantry tents, but no one had the strength to do that just now. And with hundreds of people from every kingdom standing guard, it was ironically the safest place the friends had slept in a long while.

"How are the water rations?" Aidan asked quietly, watching as a group of panting soldiers trudged their way further inside the encampment. "Enough for the men and the horses?"

Cassiel nodded wearily, stretching out his long legs. "For now. That being said, there are a few mitigating factors to consider..."

Katerina lifted her head in confusion, and her brother lowered his voice.

"In terms of rations, things are pretty cut and dried. The bad news is, we don't know how long we'll be staying. The good news is...we know not all of us will be staying."

She shook her head, just as confused. "Not all of us will be...wait. How is that good news?"

He gave her a long look. "Just in terms of water."

Suddenly, it clicked.

Yes, they might be staying in a barren wasteland for an undetermined amount of time, but in terms of rations many of the men wouldn't live to drink their share. It was a calculating sort of business, but a business, nonetheless. One that Kailas had some experience with.

"Was it like this before?" she asked quietly. "When you were hunting me?"

He glanced up suddenly, looking startled, then shook his head.

"No, I..." A moment of extreme hesitation stole his words as he shifted uncomfortably on his blanket. "You stayed in mostly forested areas. We could always replenish water and food."

She stared at him a long moment, then flashed a dry grin. "You're welcome."

"So what happens when we run out of water?" Serafina asked softly. A place like the Dunes was the complete antithesis of everything the fae needed to survive. She'd grown quieter and quieter the longer they'd ridden into the desert. "What happens when we stay here longer than we planned, and the rations run dry?"

Kailas turned away from his sister, wrapping a supportive arm around his love's waist. "Then I'll fly back to the High Kingdom and get more—"

"You absolutely will not."

The prince looked over in surprise to where Cassiel was reclining by the fire.

"Why not? The journey is days on foot, but I could make the flight in only a few hours."

The fae rolled his eyes impatiently, flashing a look that made every mortal present feel as though they were a very small child. "How many times must I say it? There are things that roam these lands *bigger* than a dragon. You shift now, one of them will pick you right out of the sky."

A memory of that three-headed beast flashed through Katerina's mind and she stifled a shudder. Her brother was plagued with the same terrifying image, yet still he tried to rally.

"But if the choice is between that and starvation—"

"Yes, we all know." Cassiel settled himself back on the ground, hands folded behind his head. "You're no longer a homicidal psychopath. Deep down, you're selfless and brave."

Kailas paled and looked away while Serafina slowly leaned forward, giving her brother a chilling look. "Say that again..."

"Come on, Sera." Cassiel's eyes sparkled as they swept over the stricken prince. "You heard him in the woods. The boy can fight his own battles."

Katerina lifted her eyebrows as Kailas glanced back in surprise. The two men locked eyes, and for a split second they looked on the verge of smiling. But Serafina wasn't finished.

"Say that again...and I'll cut off both your hands."

This time, it was Cassiel who paled and looked away.

Fortunately, at that moment, several servants arrived carrying a steaming pot, along with some spoons and bowls. One of them shook out a linen tablecloth before promptly realizing they had no table upon which to place it. They shared a stricken look, then blushed at the same time.

"My apologies, Your Majesty." The man standing in front of Katerina sank into a low bow, careful not to spill what he was holding. "It's only a simple stew—"

"Nonsense," she said kindly, taking the pot right out of his hands. "It's more than enough."

She set it on the ground between them as the servants hurried away—not understanding it was richer fare than the friends had eaten in weeks. So rich, Katerina couldn't actually look at it.

As the steam wafted into the air, she turned her face away—lying down instead.

"Are you all right?" Serafina asked in concern.

"Fine," she answered shakily. "Just feeling a little sick."

It was clearly going around. Tanya had been pale and clammy all day. Even now she was lying with her head in Cassiel's lap, eyes closed as he stroked back locks of damp hair.

"Try to get some sleep," Kailas said quietly. His eyes flickered to the company of armed men standing around them before returning to his sister. "You're safe here."

...in the Dunes.

Katerina forced a smile and nodded, forcing a few bites and urging the others to do the same. Then she settled down, pressing her head into the flat pillow.

They both knew how fast that could change...

WHEN KATERINA WOKE, it was still dark outside. She was surprised. The sun was so overpowering, a part of her thought it would never relinquish its grip on the sky. She pushed onto her elbows and glanced around. The rest of her friends were still sleeping, stretched out beside the dying fire. It was a peaceful scene, yet they looked almost frightening in the darkness. So quiet, so still. If it wasn't for the sound of their gentle breathing, she'd wonder if they were even alive.

As quietly as she could, she got up and started wandering through the campsite. Most of the guards who had been stationed around the perimeter had fallen asleep. Those whose eyes were still open didn't notice as she slipped through their ranks, heading to the small pond at the edge of camp.

The pond was the reason they'd stopped. No water for miles in the wasted desert, and yet the tiny pool of water had somehow survived the scorching sun. It was the same reason all the traders had stopped there before them. The same reason they'd decided to stay for the night.

Not that it was drinkable. The badlands had earned its name for a reason. Everything inside bred pestilence and death. Chances were, the little pond would prove no exception. Not even the horses had been allowed to try.

Still, it had a surprisingly calming effect as she sank to her knees beside the rushes, trailing a stick in the waves. It rippled just like regular water. Made the same cheery splashing sound. For all she knew, it wasn't poisoned at all. It was the last remnant of good before the end of the world.

She let out a quiet sigh, dropping the stick to the bottom.

Everything felt different, yet eerily familiar. Facing certain death, but with an army of people at her side. Sleeping beside a campfire with her friends, but with one very important person missing.

...where are you?

She tilted her head towards the moon, but couldn't see it through the haze. The light was obscured, and she could only imagine where it might have been from the long stretching shadows.

Dylan would be making a joke right now, she thought miserably. *He would be trying to cheer me up.*

It didn't matter what crisis they were facing, the ranger never played by the odds. He could be trapped in a Carpathian dungeon or up to his neck in a Burgaten swamp, but the man was pure charisma. It was what had drawn Katerina to him in the first place—that secret twinkle in his eyes.

Then the blade pierced his skin...and that twinkle vanished.

A leaded weight crept into her arms, dropping them limp to her sides as she replayed every word that had been said back in the castle.

While everyone gathered had appeared to be shocked at the use of a *doronos* blade, none of them seemed to have the slightest doubt what would happen next. The enchanted dagger could take a life just as surely as any other. It just left the body behind to gloat.

She remembered the way Michael shut down when he heard it. The way Cassiel flew into a rage, coming to the ranger's defense. Under most circumstances, it would have been a comfort. But she had known the fae long enough to see the panic in his eyes.

Are you really gone? That moment in the cave...was it really goodbye?

If only she could see him again, just for moment. One moment and she'd be able to tell if there was anything left to salvage. Any trace of the man she loved behind those blue eyes.

She sat on her heels, leaning over the shimmering pool. For a second, she almost didn't recognize the face staring back at her. The watery reflection was too tired, too pale. The kind of girl who should be home sick in bed, not marching with a magical army to the end of the world.

The tips of her hair touched the surface as she leaned even closer, squinting to get a better look. Had there always been such bruises un-

der her eyes? Such gaunt hollows in her cheeks? She tilted her head this
way and that. Such a sad face for a girl who was supposed to be queen.

Then, all at once...another face appeared in the reflection.

It was like a punch to the stomach.

The world ceased to matter. Time screeched to a stop. For a split
second, all the trembling queen could do was stare. Then her lips parted
ever so slightly as she turned around.

"...Dylan?"

He stepped back quickly as she pushed to her feet, the way a wild
animal would spook when you moved too suddenly. One foot had angled back the way he'd come, but when he saw her truly dumbstruck
expression he couldn't help but smile—lifting a finger to his lips.

"Shh...I'm not supposed to be here."

Her knees trembled and locked. She had no idea how she was still
standing. "But...but you *are* here."

She couldn't believe the words coming out of her own mouth; it
was as if she'd stumbled into some kind of dream. With a gasp of happiness she took a lurching step forward, only to have him step away just
as quickly.

"Dylan, you escaped!"

Ever since that three-headed beast carried him off into the sky, she'd
been completely unable to say his name. Now, she couldn't stop saying
it. Every deadened part of her body seemed to come back to life, light-
ing up with the very sound.

"You're here!"

She couldn't stop smiling. She was so overwhelmed, she'd yet to realize that he hadn't really spoken himself. That he was keeping a careful
barrier of space.

Another set of tears slipped down her face, and his eyes softened
with a hint of sympathy.

"It doesn't work that way, my love."

Her breathing faltered as the smile froze on her face. Why wasn't he happier? Why wasn't he rushing towards her? After everything that happened, he couldn't still be angry about the kiss.

"What do you mean?" She lifted her hands towards him, noticing for the first time as he pulled away. "Dylan, why are you—"

"Haven't you heard?" His lips twitched into a sarcastic smile. "I'm bewitched."

There was a hitch in her breathing as her arms slowly lowered to her sides. So he hadn't escaped the power of the dagger after all. But then, how had he managed to escape?

"I didn't escape," he said quietly, as if reading her thoughts. Those lovely blue eyes glowed silver in the moon, somehow catching the light even through the desert haze. "I was sent to you."

...by him.

For the very first time since seeing him, a tiny shiver of fear swept over her skin. She'd dealt with enchanted people before. If it wasn't Cassiel trying to hack them all to pieces in Laurelwood Forest then it was the cannibalistic villagers or her twin brother, bewitched against her all these years. She'd seen people she'd trust with her life turn against her without a second thought.

Such was the power of sorcery.

She didn't ask why he was sent. A part of her wasn't able to do that just yet. A part of her was still fighting not to throw herself into his arms. She asked a different question instead.

"So...you're not going to stay?"

Her voice hitched halfway through as the question scraped through her throat like shards of glass. He *had* to stay. He was standing *right there*. He couldn't possibly go back.

"I could." For the first time he took a step towards her, an emotion she'd never seen flickering tentatively in his eyes. "I could stay right here. It's entirely your decision."

Her mind flashed back to that moment with the Knight—the offer she'd made.

"Me for you," she said breathlessly. "Is that it? You can stay, if I go in your place?"

Before he could answer, she began hasty preparations: tightening the cord on her cloak, the laces on her shoes, wishing again she'd had something more to eat.

"That's fine," she said quickly, as if the offer was likely to expire. "That's just fine. Obviously I won't have time to tell the others where I went, but you can do that for me."

"Katerina—"

"If you wouldn't mind doing it *after* I'm gone, that would be great."

She didn't think her friends would take kindly to the fact that she'd snuck off in the middle of the night and offered herself as a sacrificial lamb. Chances were, they'd launch an instant rescue party and end up dragging her back by the hair.

"Katerina, would you—"

"So how will it work in terms of the enchantment?" she asked in that same rushed voice. "Is it the kind of thing that will wear off of you once I pass a certain line? Or do I have to stab the blade into myself to get it all out of your system—"

"Would you *listen* to me?"

There was a harsh edge to his voice she'd never heard before. One that contrasted strangely with the serene expression on his face. He was watching her scramble, but it didn't seem to make a difference. He was watching her crying, but he didn't seem to care. It was as if there was an invisible pane of glass between them. None of the emotions were getting through.

She fell quiet, staring nervously into his eyes.

"I was sent to you with an offer," he said calmly. "But it isn't for your life, it's to save mine."

That was *good* news. She had to keep telling herself. It was good news, because it meant there was still a life to save. And there was nothing she wouldn't do to save it. It was *good* news.

...then why did it give her chills?

"All right," she said slowly, staring into his eyes, "...what is it?"

He waited a moment, then smiled.

It was the cruelest thing to happen yet. Because, for a moment, she saw the man she'd fallen in love with. For a moment, everything was the way it had been before. Like there had never been a kiss, or a cave, or an enchanted blade. As if they were simply two people standing beneath the stars.

"It's simple...my life for the pendant."

The moment vanished into the haze.

Her jaw slowly fell open as she stared at him. Unable to believe her ears. Because, while it may have sounded like a simple exchange, the fate of the five kingdoms rested on her next words.

"Your life..."

"...for the pendant," he finished the sentence for her, offering yet another devastating smile.

She stared at him a moment then lowered her eyes, trying to gather her thoughts.

The pendant—he may as well have asked for the realm. Because that's what they were really talking about. Whoever held the pendant could tip the scales in the battle yet to come. If she were to surrender it to the Knight for *any* price...all those people sleeping in the trees would be lost.

"I don't want to rush you," he said with a hint of humor, "but I don't want to be standing here when the rest of them wake up either. What will it be, Katerina? Are you going to send me back into the wasteland? Or can I stay here with you?"

Her lips parted as a river of new tears streamed down her face. For a moment, she was simply speechless. Then she dug her nails into her hand and forced herself to take a breath.

"...you want me to do this?"

The Dylan she knew would say no. The Dylan she knew would be screaming it at the top of his lungs. But the man in front of her was different. There was a chance she didn't know him at all.

He didn't quite answer, but answered all the same.

"I didn't know what it would be like when we landed at the castle. All my life I'd heard stories, but..." A shiver ran over his body as he glanced towards the horizon, his eyes shining with fear. "The things he-the things he's made me do..."

A truly heartbreaking expression crashed over him as their eyes met in the dark.

"Katerina...*please*."

The young queen stood perfectly still, as if a sudden paralysis had taken hold.

Every instinct was screaming to save him. Her hands were aching to tear the glowing pendant right off her neck and throw it to the ground at his feet.

What did she care if he gave it to the Knight? What did she care if the five kingdoms burned to the ground, as long as the man she loved was standing beside her?

Then a line creased in the center of her brow, and she tilted her head to the side.

"Why did you call me that?"

He faltered a moment, staring warily across the grass. "...what?"

"Katerina." She took a sudden step forward, and he took a sudden step back. "You keep saying Katerina, but you never call me that. You always call me Katy."

There was a beat of silence. Then he smiled.

"Katy..." He held out his hand, beckoning her towards him. His eyes danced with the light of the ruby, but the smile stayed fixed on his face. "Please do this for me."

His voice lowered to a tender whisper.

"...then we can be together."

For a second she reached towards him, lost in those impossible blue eyes. Then she turned up her hand, pointing her glowing palm directly at his heart.

"You never call me Katy."

In a flash, everything changed.

The smile sharpened on his face as the arm reaching for her suddenly lengthened. His chest broadened and his hair became streaked with grey as the silvery blue melted out of his eyes. A second later the ranger had vanished completely, and a different man was standing in his place. A man who threw his head back with a deep rumble of booming laughter.

"Very clever, sweetheart. And I thought I had you fooled."

She recoiled from him, like a child jerking back from a snake. "You're sick."

He laughed again, loud and long, completely unconcerned with who might hear him. It was a dangerous gamble, especially considering the army sleeping just a few paces beyond. But no one came running. The desert was quiet and cold.

"I'm *bored*," he corrected, staring down with a twinkle of amusement. "Waiting for you and your little army to make their way across the Dunes. I never imagined it would take so long."

She inched backwards until her feet touched the edge of the pond. "You've waited this many years, what's a few more days?"

He smiled again, baring each one of his teeth.

"You know, that's *exactly* what your boyfriend said at dinner last night. Usually he's so quiet, but I've found there are ways to get him to speak."

An arc of fire shot out of her palms, missing his head by just inches. If he hadn't ducked at precisely the right moment, it would have gone right through the center of his face.

"He also said *that* might happen." The towering man straightened up, chuckling under his breath. "Apparently, you've got a bit of a temper."

Katerina froze where she stood, glaring with all her might. "Why did you come here? You can't think I'm just going to *give* you the pendant."

He tilted his head, as though considering it for the first time. Then his lips widened into another hair-raising smile. "No, I don't imagine you would. Not even to spare his life."

Her spine stiffened, but she didn't give an inch of ground. "His life was never on the line. It was you all along—"

"Sweet girl," he interrupted quietly, "do you really think that's true? Do you really think he's safe, when you let him go home with someone like me?"

She tried to answer, but the words stuck in her throat.

"Your little king answers to me now. He goes where I tell him. Shifts when I tell him. Kills who I tell him to kill." He took a step closer, blocking out what was left of the light. "Do you really think, at the end of this story, I won't tell him to kill you?"

All at once, the image in front of her changed. She no longer saw the Knight, and the pond, and the little oasis. The place around her looked almost like a tomb. A dark fortress made of stone sealed so tight, there was no way for light to get through.

A single torch shone in the room. And there, sitting just beneath it, was a man very much like the one she used to know. Same build, same clothes, same tangle of dark hair falling into his eyes. But the similarities stopped there. This man was too pale, too damaged. At a glance he looked almost like a beautiful corpse, reanimated to sit quietly by himself in the dark.

A violent noise sounded deep in the castle and he lifted his eyes in dread. A second later, he shivered and wrapped his arms around his knees, bowing his head into his chest.

"What have you done to him?!" Katerina shrieked, coming back to the clearing and throwing herself at the Knight in a rage. "Tell me what you—"

"Careful, child." He caught her easily by the wrists, holding her at bay. "We don't want you hurting yourself. Not yet."

She tried shooting another wave of fire, but found she no longer had the strength. Instead she sank to her knees, shaking uncontrollably.

"What have you done to him?" she whispered again.

No matter where she looked, she kept seeing him. Barefoot and without a cloak to protect him from the cold. Huddled beneath the torch, a look of childlike fear shining in his eyes.

The Knight knelt down in front of her with an unexpectedly gentle expression. "Nothing the pendant wouldn't fix."

When she finally lifted her eyes, he held out an open hand. "Give it to me...and I'll give him back to you."

Why doesn't he just take it? It's not like I could stop him.

The man was kneeling just a few inches away. Close enough that he could reach out one of those massive hands and snap her neck. It wouldn't be a stretch to steal her mother's necklace. Why ask for it? Unless...he'd come that night looking for something else.

"What do really want?" she asked, straightening up as best she could. "You didn't come here for the necklace. And you had to know I'd never give it to you. Dylan wouldn't want that."

"But you want Dylan."

There was a hitch in her breathing.

"I asked you a question."

His lips twitched into a smile.

"He's right. You have a bit of a temper." In a fluid motion he pushed to his feet, gesturing to the camp at the same time. "I'll admit, I was curious. It's been a long time since I..."

He trailed off, eyes flickering over the sparse trees.

"Ah, but this is too easy," he mused. "I think I'll send a little welcome present to you and your friends. Give them a taste of things to come."

Katerina pushed to her feet with a shiver, glancing around in the dark.

"What do you—"

"You won't want to miss this." He dropped a heavy hand on her shoulder, giving her a firm shake. "You'll want to wake up."

She blinked up at him, unable to move.

"...what?"

He shook her again, even harder this time.

"You heard me—"

All of a sudden, his voice changed into someone else's.

"—wake up!"

KATERINA'S TEETH CHATTERED together as her head knocked against the ground. All at once, the cool night air vanished and she realized she was drenched in sweat. Two hands were clamped around her upper arms, shaking with increasing panic. She flinched and tried to open her eyes.

"That's it—stay with me! Open your eyes!"

Twice, the world blinked into focus. But she was blinded by light. Faces floated into view, but she couldn't identify them. She didn't understand why she was lying on the ground.

"...it's hot," she mumbled.

At once, she was pulled off the ground—laid across someone's knees. Cool hands appeared from nowhere, placing something cold and wet on her forehead. More hands were unlacing her cloak. A voice shouted in a language she didn't understand.

"Dylan?"

She didn't know whether she'd spoken out loud. He'd been there, hadn't he? They'd been standing together beside the water?

There was a pause as the faces turned to each other, sharing a look she'd never see.

"Kat, do you know where you are? Can you see me?"

Is that Tanya?

The young queen lifted a hand weakly in the air, groping for what might have been the silhouetted tips of spiky hair, before giving up in exhaustion.

"...should have eaten more of the soup."

"What's happening to her?" Her twin brother's voice broke through the mental fog, wild with panic. "This isn't heat exhaustion—she's delirious!"

"Give her some space to breathe," Serafina calmed him gently. "Aidan, can you heal her?"

"I don't think so." The vampire's musical voice was close, just inches away. He must have been the one holding her. "It doesn't work on everything...and this?"

"What even happened?!" Kailas demanded again, shaking free of his girlfriend's restraining hands. "You were just talking to her, and then—"

"Look at that! Her shoe is torn."

There was a flash of white hair as Cassiel knelt at her side, hastily untangling the laces before pulling it off her foot. He turned it over in gentle hands before stopping suddenly. The group flinched at the same time as they saw the tiny wound, two small holes in the side of her heel.

"Two punctures," Tanya murmured. "That's not a scorpion..."

"No," Serafina replied grimly. "That's something else."

In a move that would forever baffle her, Cassiel lifted Katerina's foot to his lips—almost as if he was kissing it. There was a soft tugging sensation, then he spat out a mouthful of blood.

"It's already in her system," he panted. "It's too late to draw it out."

"What does that mean?!" Kailas sank down between the fae and the vampire, too panicked to maintain the barrier of space he usually kept between them. "You can't just give up—"

"I'm not giving up," Cassiel said calmly, moving the prince aside. There was a gentle lurch as the vampire vanished and she was pulled into a different set of arms. "She's opened her eyes—that means she's through the worst of it. We just need to get her through the rest."

Serafina shot him a quick glance, but held her tongue.

"Katerina."

She struggled to focus at the sound of the fae's stern voice. It reminded her of their sparring practice at the monastery. He'd been a good teacher—but tough.

Two hands gripped the sides of her face. She was momentarily shaded from the sun.

"I need you to blink three times. Can you do that for me?"

Doubtful.

Blinking required energy. It also required counting. It also required...

...what did he ask me?

"Kat, I need you to focus." A face floated into her line of sight, capturing her drifting attention. "Blink three times."

She blinked many more times than that, staring up at him in wonder.

It was as if she'd never really looked at Cassiel until that day. Backlit by the desert sun, glowing like some heavenly king. Her mouth fell open in shock as she lifted a hand to his face.

"...you're like an angel."

There was some quiet laughter behind her. The fae gentled with a tender smile.

"See? She's making sense already."

Only one person failed to see the humor. Kailas quickly reclaimed his place by the fae's side, reaching straight over him to hold his sister's hands. "Are you all right? Say something—please."

It was impossible not to be moved by the fear in his voice. Too many times in the last few days, the prince had seen his sister hovering on the brink of death. Four dazed words were not enough to ease that apprehension.

"Katy," he pleaded, leaning closer, "talk to me."

There was a split second of silence.

...*Katy.*

Then it all came flooding back.

In a flash the queen was pushing to her feet, fighting against the arms that restrained her. It was a task made all the more difficult by her lack of balance and solitary shoe, but she tried anyway.

"Let go!" she gasped. "We have to get out of here!"

Cassiel tried to soothe her, ignoring the hands pounding against his chest.

"It's all right, honey—just take a breath." He shifted deliberately to block the boisterous army, trying to calm her down. "You were bitten by a spider. You've been hallucinating."

"A spider?" Kailas asked in surprise.

Serafina nodded, speaking under her breath. "I've seen it before. Vareezi spider venom causes delirium and hallucinations. Most people don't come out of it..."

"No, you don't understand!" Katerina continued fighting, twisting and turning with all her might to get free. "The Red Knight was here—he has Dylan! He's sending something this way—"

"It was in your mind," Aidan soothed, standing beside Cassiel to catch her eyes. "You and I were speaking just a few seconds ago. Then, suddenly, you collapsed."

...a few seconds...

In a daze, Katerina stopped her struggles long enough to stare around—squinting in the bright afternoon sun. She couldn't believe it. There was no oasis. No pond, no makeshift camp. She could still see the tracks she and Aidan had made in the sand.

"But..." She trailed off, staring at the ground in confusion. A second later, her legs gave out and she sank noiselessly into Cassiel's arms. "We never slept? We never made it to the pond?"

The fae and the vampire exchanged a quick look before Cassiel shook his head.

"There is no pond, Kat. There's no water in this part of the realm."

She stared up at him in confusion, still feeling the little waves on her heels. "But it was so real..." she murmured. "I remember the smell of the campfire. The feel of the evening sun on my face. Dylan was there, and he..."

She trailed off again, unwilling to go any further.

"You never had a fight?" In an effort to shift the conversation, she gestured between the fae and her brother. "You never teased him for being a homicidal psychopath?"

The two men shared a quick look then Cassiel turned back to her, all seriousness.

"Why would I joke about that? It's a serious condition."

"He said no such thing," Serafina interrupted, swatting her brother impatiently. "I would have cut off both his hands," she added as an afterthought.

Katerina gave her a long look, feeling more and more off-balance.

"Yeah...that's what you said..."

"It was a dream, Kat." Tanya squeezed her hands, looking just as worn out as she had the day they left the castle. "Just a dream."

The queen tried to nod, but stopped when she felt a sharp burn on her chest. The pendant was glowing fiercely, shining right through her gown. Instead, she turned her eyes to Aidan.

"But can't dreams serve as a warning?" she asked quietly. "A prophecy of things to come?"

He stared at her curiously, those dark eyes lost in thought.

"Sometimes..." he began slowly. "But usually to those ordained with the gift. True prophecy is incredibly rare, and if you've never—"

"Not me," she interrupted, grabbing the pendant. "*This.*"

As one, the six friends looked down at the fiery ruby before lifting their heads.

"I'm telling you...something's coming."

That's when they heard the first of the screams.

Chapter 7

There was no time to react. There was no time to do anything but watch as the swarm of creatures flooded over the sand, descending upon the stalled army.

There was no time to put on armor.

At first, it was hard to even tell what they were. Smaller than a wolf, but more compact. Built closer to a bear. They ran on all fours with incredible speed, their serrated claws leaving jagged lines in the sand. Patches of tawny brown fur made them almost impossible to see until they were right on top of you, but by then all you could notice were the teeth. Row upon row of glistening fangs.

"Take cover!" Cassiel shouted.

But it was already too late. The desert erupted in screams as the savage beasts tore through their ranks. Ripping and slashing as they went. Never slowing their speed.

Hyenas, Katerina realized as one of them went tearing past her. *They're like hyenas.*

No sooner had she thought the word than the world exploded in shrieking laughter. An eerie, high-pitched yipping that seemed to come from the beasts themselves.

Her hands flew over her mouth as one of them leapt upon a knight of the High Kingdom, ripping out his throat before he could even raise his sword. He was still falling as five more jumped upon a lone wolf—thrashing around for a moment before tearing it to shreds.

"Can you stand?"

She whipped around to see Cassiel staring down at her, one hand wrapped tightly around her arm. When she was too disoriented to answer he doubled his grip, shouting the question again.

"Katerina, can you stand!"

No, probably not.

"Y-yes," she stammered, glancing down at her trembling knees. "I'll be fine."

He gave her another measured look then released her, reaching up in the same motion to pull an arrow from the quiver on his back. Within seconds, twelve of the snarling beasts fell dead to the ground. The sand soaked up the blood before it could pool. Four seconds and twelve perfect shots. But the fae was out of arrows. And the beasts were starting to swarm their way.

"Get behind me!" he shouted, reaching up to pull two silver swords from his back.

They flashed in the sunlight as he gave them a cursory twirl, but the queen wasn't one to hide in the shadows. A moment later, she was standing by his side.

Their eyes met and she flashed a humorless smile.

"Get behind me."

His eyes flickered to her glowing palms before returning quickly to the pack of mutts flying their way. "That fire better be working, Your Majesty. You're not dreaming anymore."

A wave of liquid flame shot inches above his head, incinerating five at a time.

"I'm clear on that—thanks."

Together they drove a line of them back, working with the synchronicity of two people who'd been fighting together for a long time. One would go on the offensive while the other would cover. One would aim high as the other went low. It was a stunning display of power, between the fae's flashing swords and the queen's spiraling waves of fire.

But it was only a matter of time before a scream pierced the air.

In a heartbeat, Cassiel stopped what he was doing—staring back the way they'd come. A trio of beasts took advantage of his distraction to leap straight towards him, but the queen drove them back with another spray of flames. He didn't even notice, as his gaze was lost in the crowd.

"What is it?" she gasped breathlessly, covering for him again as he froze motionless amidst the bloody fray. "What's wrong?"

He stood there a second more, then he found what he was looking for.

"...Tanya."

He left without another word, flying over the sand with such speed that Katerina didn't even see what was happening until he was already gone.

"Cass—"

She tried to call after him, but was instantly overrun. The creatures they were fighting didn't have much intelligence, but they made up for it with raw instinct. The second there was an opening, they swarmed forward to fill the gap. The second she was alone, they closed in for the kill.

"Stupid, ungrateful, disloyal, treacherous fae," she hissed between her teeth.

A pair of silver arrows flew into the eyes of a beast leaping towards her, and she turned around to see an immortal warrior standing with a bow behind her back. Their eyes met for a split second before she grimaced a guilty apology.

"...I take it back."

The fae was knocked to the ground a moment later, letting out a sharp cry as a ravenous hyena sank its teeth deep into his pale neck. The hyena was dead a second later. But so was the fae.

Katerina stared in shock at his handsome face—eyes staring lifelessly at the sky, blonde hair staining slowly with blood. Then a searing pain raked down the sides of her arms.

"Seven hells!"

In a daze of pain, she turned around to see a snarling beast slowly circling around her. It stood as tall as her chin and, judging by the deep gashes and arrows sticking out of its hide, people had tried and failed to kill it many times before. Its lips pulled back in a grisly sort of smile as it stalked low to the ground. The fire flickered dangerously, but wouldn't light in her injured hands.

With a frightened gasp she looked around for anything she could use as a weapon, taking a blood-soaked sword right out of the dead fae's hand. It felt cold and unnatural in her fingers. The grip was hard to keep hold of, whether from the seamless silver or the rivers of blood.

In an act of desperation she pulled off a strip of her dress and wrapped it around the handle, keeping her eyes on the creature the whole time. It wouldn't be enough to stop it. She knew that full well. But for one of the first times, none of her friends was close enough to help her.

Kailas and Serafina had been separated to the side of the bat-tle—she could see streaks of fire along with the flash of a silver sword far across the sand. The vampire had been driven in the opposite direc-tion—fighting off many more than his share while trying to make his way back to the rest of them at the same time. That just left Cassiel and Tanya, but for the life of her Katerina wasn't able to find them. And her time had finally run out.

The hyena sank low into a crouch, shaking its head back and forth with that wild, haunting laughter. She dug her feet into the sand and tightened her grip on the blade, eyes narrowing into a fierce glare. If this creature was to kill her, she'd make it remember for the rest of time.

But just as it leapt into the air...something even stronger knocked it down again.

What?!

The queen stumbled back in surprise as a silver-grey wolf flew out of nowhere, leaping high enough to tackle the foul creature right out of the air. They landed with a sharp impact, but no sooner had they touched the ground than they were up and fighting again. Ripping into each other with unnatural savagery and lethal, merciless claws.

It didn't take long. The hyenas may have been able to overwhelm a single shifter with sheer numbers, but there was very little that could beat a wolf on its own.

Within seconds the creature was on the ground, torn straight through the middle.

Katerina watched as every drop of blood in its body poured into the parched sand; as the life flickered suddenly, then vanished from its eyes. She took a second to catch her breath, then turned around to thank her unlikely savior...only to find that the wolf was not alone.

She stared in astonishment as another shifter flew out of the crowd. Followed by another, and another, and another after that. Within a matter of seconds, almost the entire Belarian army was standing in a tight circle around her—fencing her off from the battle in an impenetrable wall of fur.

It seemed Dylan had left very careful instructions before he left.

The girl he loved was to be protected at all costs.

For a few seconds, she simply stood there. She couldn't see much of what was going on around her. The wolves hadn't even left her much room to move. But she could hear the screams still echoing from the battle, and with a burst of strength she tried to break free.

"Let me out!" she demanded, struggling against the wolf standing directly in front of her. It was a valiant effort, but the thing didn't even move. "Let me out—I command you!"

The wolf stared back at her calmly as its brethren continued the bloody fight. There wasn't a hint of fear in its eyes, nor was there a hint of compromise. She may have been a queen, but he took orders from a king. And those orders had been painfully clear.

Besides, she wouldn't recognize them once they shifted back into men. How could she hold this one man accountable for disobedience, when she didn't know his face?

There was also the fact that her own council fervently supported the surge of protection.

Since the first of the wretched hyenas had flown over the desert sand, Abel Bishop and the Knights of the High Kingdom had been fighting to protect their queen. It was a job made all the more difficult by the fact that she'd been standing so far in front of the rest of the army when the attack occurred. With every swing of their swords they'd been trying desperately to reach her, but all those struggles stopped the second they saw she was protected by the wolves.

A silent understanding passed between them. A silent look of thanks.

Then they turned back to the battle with renewed vengeance.

If the five kingdoms hadn't exactly been united before, they certainly were now. The Knights of the High Kingdom had rallied together beside the Fae and formed a sort of coalition. Men fought with swords in front while the immortal archers stood tall beside them, firing arrows with deadly precision through the cracks in their ranks. On the other side of the field, the witches were fighting in a similar way with Petra's rebels. A tight-knit circle had climbed upon the carcasses of those already killed and were firing balls of multi-colored light into the crowd. Shifters and goblins were working in tandem. Men and warlocks were fighting side by side.

Michael had probably taken out about a quarter of the enemy all by himself, heaving a sword as long as Katerina's body, laying waste to everything in his path.

There was a high-pitched cry and she snapped back to the present, whirling around to see the severed head of a hyena flying through the air. It was followed quickly by three others. The queen stood on the tips of her toes and saw Petra whirling a javelin at the speed of light. The ancient general seemed almost to be smiling. A second later, Katerina realized why.

The battle was done. The hyenas just didn't know it yet.

They moved less like a pack and more like a battering ram—not seeming to care what damage was inflicted upon themselves, as long as they were able to force their way through. But they didn't have the numbers, and the armies of the five kingdoms had them surrounded—herding them towards a particular point. It took Katerina a moment to realize where that point was.

The wolves of Belaria weren't to be taken lightly. And behind the lupine muscles and snarling teeth, there was a mind at work. The second the remaining creatures thundered their way they surged together like a kind of wave—one leaping off the back of another, launching themselves wildly into the air. There was a series of high-pitched cries as that wicked laughter changed into something different. Something no longer cruel and scornful. Something that sounded like the end.

But before the final creature could be dispatched...a horn sounded in the distance.

As one, every person fighting in the sand turned their heads—gazing silently towards the distant Dunes. They couldn't see whoever had called, but the message was clear.

It was time to retreat.

The hyenas shifted momentum on a dime and barreled through the remaining army at breakneck speed, never slowing until they'd vanished into the desert haze.

The soldiers looked around at each other in confusion, slowly lowering their weapons to their sides. It was a clear victory, but everyone still standing knew the retreat was only temporary.

They'd encountered only a small portion of the Knight's army.

And it had already come at a cost...

A sudden hush swept through the crowd, the sound of a thousand whispering voices suddenly going silent. Katerina turned to see where they were looking, then saw a group of men on horseback gathered in a tight circle, staring at something lying on the ground.

The horses hadn't fared well in the fight, but it wasn't a horse they were staring at. It was a rider. A terribly familiar rider with a look of surprise permanently affixed to his handsome face.

Henry Chambers, Lord of the Horsemen of Vale, was dead.

Chapter 8

There was no way to hold a proper funeral in the desert. Not *that* desert. A land so wasted and evil that no one could bear the thought of leaving their beloved friend behind. His body was set on fire instead. A custom Katerina had found borderline barbaric, until she saw it with her own eyes.

She stood in a solemn line with the others, watching as two of the famed horsemen slowly walked forward—each holding a torch by their side. There was something similar about their faces, a familial resemblance that mirrored the man lying on the pyre. She wondered if they were his sons.

"Do you remember the first time we met him?" Tanya asked quietly. Despite the heat, she was wrapped in a thick cloak. Her hands shivered slightly as she pulled it tighter. "When he walked into the infirmary after fishing us out of Laurelwood?"

"He went back inside for me and Dylan," Cassiel replied softly. "No one who'd entered the forest had ever come out alive, but he went inside...for two people he didn't even know."

Katerina's chest tightened as she forced a watery smile. "He kept trying to get us to drop the formalities and call him Henry."

The three friends warmed at the memory, then saddened at the same time.

They'd fought battles before, buried friends and spilled blood. They'd known when they set out for the Dunes that some of their number wouldn't be coming back. But there was something particularly heartbreaking about the scene in front of them. That Henry would be the first to fall.

In perfect unison, the young men lifted the torches to the funeral pyre—setting the entire thing ablaze. Silent tears poured down their faces as the flames danced higher and higher. After a few moments the older put his arm around the younger, leading him away.

"Seventeen-hundred." Aidan walked up behind them, digging his hands into his pockets as the smoke drifted up into the sky. "That's how many we lost."

His hands were torn and the front of his shirt was soaked in blood. Unlike the others, he'd fought the beasts on his own. When his sword was knocked away, he'd been forced to use his fangs.

"We're lucky it wasn't more," Serafina murmured, glancing back at the demoralized troops stacking funeral pyres of their own. "They were already tired and weary from the sun."

"Or suffering from hallucinations of their own..." Aidan added softly, shooting a secret glance at the young queen. More specifically, to the ruby pendant glowing around her neck.

She wasn't the only one to have been bitten by a venomous spider. She wasn't the only one seeing things the others were not. But she was the only one to have prophesized what was coming.

Katerina turned away from the smoldering pyre, unable to look a second more.

"Dylan commanded his wolves to protect me," she said quietly, oblivious to the vampire's curious stare. "The second they fought their way across the sand they had me surrounded."

The others glanced over briefly, but weren't surprised. Cassiel even offered a quick smile.

"It's because of your pendant—that's the reason he gave to the council. You needed the extra protection so the pendant wouldn't fall into the Knight's hands."

His eyes flickered to Tanya, wishing he could make the same demand and clasp that golden chain around her neck. But the words triggered a dark memory in Katerina's mind.

"...into the Knight's hands," she repeated faintly.

One part of her hallucination had been proven true—why wouldn't the rest of it? If they'd received a 'welcoming present' just as she'd predicted, couldn't the man's offer be valid as well?

"He tried to make me a deal. Dylan's life for the pendant."

The others froze at the same time, then turned around slowly. Five pairs of eyes burned into her as she pulled in a deep breath, trying to meet their gaze.

"What did you say?" Cassiel asked sharply.

At this point, she didn't know what he'd want her to say. At this point, she didn't know why it was relevant. The man was a figment of her imagination. What did it matter what she'd said?

But in the light of the funeral pyres, that 'hallucination' was carrying a bit more weight.

"...I said Dylan wouldn't want me to," she answered quietly.

The fae stiffened, as if she'd slapped him. Then nodded quickly and turned away.

For a few awkward moments, it was quiet.

Kailas was worried for his sister, Serafina was worried for her brother. Aidan was lost in thought, and Tanya was just as pale and remote as she'd been since they left the castle.

Finally, the Fae princess cleared her throat to speak. "The Knight told you they were coming? The hyenas?"

The others tensed at the same time, already dreading the inevitable answer. Those eyes shot to Katerina again, but this time she was unable to meet their gaze.

"He said it was a welcome present," she said quietly. "A taste of things to come."

Just a taste. Just one small part of his unholy army. Not even a diverse group of creatures, it was a single sect. One he didn't need. One that had already claimed seventeen-hundred lives.

The fae shared a silent look as the vampire stared deep into Katerina's eyes, almost as if he could pull the dream straight out of her mind.

As the ceremony began to disperse around them he took a sudden step forward, lowering his voice so they wouldn't be heard.

"Did he say anything else?" There was a soft urgency to his voice, one that betrayed a greater panic beneath the surface. "Even the smallest detail could—"

"That's enough, all right?"

Tanya stepped forward suddenly, shaking off her cloak at the same time. Considering the girl usually had no trouble voicing her opinions, she'd been uncharacteristically quiet since leaving the castle for the Dunes. But she more than made up for it now.

"Of *course* he didn't say anything else, otherwise Katerina would have told us. So could we all stop wasting our time with some damn hallucination and focus on the fact that we're here?" She stormed off without a backward glance, away from the army, straight through the funeral pyres to the scattered corpses that still littered the bloody field.

The others stared after her in shock, none more so than her boyfriend.

After a few seconds Katerina gave him a gentle nudge, but he shook his head—those troubled eyes locked on the shape-shifter's tiny silhouette as she stalked across the sand.

"She doesn't want me," he said softly. Katerina looked up at him in alarm and he was quick to clarify. "She doesn't want me to go after her. I've...I've already tried."

Katerina followed his worried gaze, then squeezed his shoulder. "Let me try."

SINCE DYLAN PULLED her out of the forest all those months ago, screaming denials with her hair full of leaves, Tanya Oberon had been somewhat of an enigma.

Willing to pack up her life at a moment's notice, the girl had no trouble backpacking around the five kingdoms. She also had a comically strong sense of self-preservation while, at the same time, never hesitating a moment before selflessly risking her life. A consummate loner, yet she'd found herself a family. A strict independent, yet she'd fallen in love with a fae.

When they'd found themselves in the Temple of Bones, at the heart of the Kreo jungle, all those contradictions had started to make sense. The girl was an orphan, trying to outrun the grief, endlessly moving from place to place so that heavy crown couldn't fall upon her head.

A rather convoluted life narrative, but her new friends could empathize. Better than that, they could begin to help her through it. Help her face those inner demons. Help her stand still long enough to catch her breath. With a little coaxing, one of them had even taught her to love.

As the months went by and friendship turned to family, Katerina prided herself on having earned a place closer than most. Before either one knew what was happening, she and the neurotic shape-shifter had found themselves the best of friends. She could predict the girl's actions. Guess virtually every twisted and nonsensical thing going on inside that head.

...until today.

"May I join you?"

Tanya cast her a quick look, but never stopped her manic pacing. What it was she was doing was a bit of a mystery. Going from body to body. Turning them over. Searching each one.

Katerina watched her for a moment, then decided to go out on a limb.

"...did you lose your flask?"

That produced a bit of a reaction.

Tanya's hands paused over the carcass of a fallen hyena as her lips twitched with the hint of a smile. Instead of answering, she reached deep into its ribcage and yanked as hard as she could. A second later, she thrust a bloody arrow in between them.

"We're going to need these."

The queen blinked in surprise. And *relief.* At some point in the last year, each of them had had at least one moment when they'd reached their limit. When they'd crossed the point of sanity, and the others had to tow them back to the other side.

But the arrows...made sense.

As smoke from the pyres rose in the distance Katerina knelt beside her, helping her shift the heavy bodies, grabbing hold of any discarded weapons they might find inside. It was a gruesome job, but necessary. A side of battle Katerina had never considered before.

For a while, they worked in silence. One focused on the hyenas and ever-growing pile of arrows. One shot secret, worried glances at her friend. Finally, Katerina dared to speak.

"Cassiel thinks you're angry with him." She watched Tanya very carefully for any hint of a reaction. "That you don't want him here."

There was a slight stiffening of her shoulders, a slight hitch in her breath. Then she pushed back a lock of unruly hair, bracing her feet against a bloody carcass as she pulled with all her might.

"Cass can speak for himself. He doesn't need to send you down here—"

"You think he sent me?" Katerina interrupted with a hint of humor. "You think that Cassiel trusted me to speak for him? The man tried to hire me a governess back at the castle. Said that Dylan and I couldn't take care of ourselves..."

She stumbled into the name without thinking, pictured his face without meaning to. For a moment, her chest ached so intensely she wasn't able to breathe.

Tanya stopped what she was doing, looking up slowly. "I'm *really* sorry about what happened to him."

Since that moment in the cave, almost everyone had said it. Since opening her eyes in the castle, almost everyone had said it again. But this was somehow worse.

Her best friend. Arms-deep in a hyena.

It suddenly became real.

He's gone. People are consoling me...because Dylan is gone.

"It's not like he died," she muttered, pushing back waves of her hair without realizing she was streaking her face in blood. "He was stabbed in the shoulder. People survive that."

Tanya watched her for a moment, then put down the arrow she was holding.

"That hallucination you had with the spider...that wasn't the whole thing, was it?"

At first Katerina started to deny it. Then she bit her lip and shook her head. Tanya's face softened as she abandoned the pile of arrows entirely and came to sit by the queen's side.

"Dylan was there?"

Katerina froze a moment, then pulled in a deep breath. "Dylan was the one who approached me...then I realized it was the Knight in disguise."

Tanya's lips parted in horror. "He disguised himself as Dylan? *Talked* to you as Dylan?"

The queen nodded slowly, processing it for the first time. "He asked me to give up the pendant, so that we could be together," she said softly. "He held out his hand...begged me to save his life."

It was quiet for a long time. Then, to Katerina's extreme astonishment, Tanya let out a single breath of laughter. When the two girls locked eyes, the shifter shook her head with a wry grin.

"Begged for his life? That doesn't sound like Dylan."

Katerina stared at her a second more, then couldn't help smiling herself. "No...it doesn't."

They sat there a while longer, staring out over the field of dead monsters, lost in thought. A few minutes went past, then Tanya graciously offered her first dibs of a decapitated hyena and the laughter began anew. It was quiet; borderline hysterical. But it was laughter, nonetheless.

Once he saw they were smiling, Cassiel slowly made his way across the sand. His hands were buried deep in his pockets, and for one of the first times since the three of them had met he looked uncharacteristically unsure. He lingered a few feet away, eyes trained on his girlfriend.

"Mind if I join you?"

Even his voice was uncertain. Nervous—despite the calm façade. His dark eyes swept over the mess of bodies before coming up blank.

"I've always loved...organ harvesting."

Katerina pushed to her feet with a grin, thrusting a handful of arrows toward him. A good deal of raw flesh went with them, and he made a visible effort not to flinch.

"*Arrow* harvesting," she corrected with a wink. "It seems your girlfriend wants to make sure you're well supplied for the next round of whatever comes over those hills."

Cassiel glanced up with a tentative smile, but the second she saw him Tanya shut back down again. Her body went rigid, her eyes distant and remote.

The fae was completely lost. "Sweetheart, could I talk to you for a—"

"I've got to get these back."

In a quick motion she pushed to her feet, grabbing the stack of arrows out of his hands and marching back towards the army. He stared after her in silence as Katerina froze in between.

"She's just...I think she's just really tired..." The queen trailed off at the look on his lovely face. There was no anger. At this point, there wasn't even much confusion. He was wistfully, heartbreakingly sad.

"I'm losing her," he said softly. In over five hundred years, it was the first time he'd found himself saying the words. "I think perhaps I've lost her already."

Katerina took a step towards him, then stopped in her tracks.

What could she possibly say? She didn't know why, but it looked like he was right. And there was a dark truth to the words that sent chills rocketing up her spine.

I'm losing him. I think perhaps I've lost him already...

BETWEEN THE SCORES of wounded and the fact that no one who'd lost a friend seemed ready to leave behind the bodies, the various high-ranking officers decided to make camp for the night.

Considering how slowly time moved during the day, transitions were impossibly abrupt in the desert. The second the sun slipped below the horizon, the land was cloaked in shadow. It was too fast for most people's eyes to adjust, too fast to begin making the fires for supper. As Katerina gazed out over the darkened hills, she wondered if the sudden darkness was a part of the Dunes themselves. Yet another superfluous danger to lure travelers and merchants to an early death.

"Kat, come get something to eat."

She turned around to see Aidan and Cassiel sitting beside a crackling fire. Tanya had decided to dine with her grandmother instead, and Kailas and Serafina were looking after the wounded. Just a few drops of the remaining fairy tonic, and even the most grisly of wounds had healed almost instantaneously. Those people who hadn't come round to the prince already were well on their way.

"Look at him," Cassiel murmured, staring across the field to where the young couple was kneeling beside a mutilated shifter, gently tilting back his head. "Buying their love."

Aidan glanced up with the hint of a smile, leaning against a bag of supplies. "Would you rather he let them die?"

Cassiel kept his eyes on the fire. "...at least it would be consistent."

The vampire made a commendable effort not to roll his eyes, while taking a stick of meat from the fae's hand and offering it out to the queen. "Finish it up. With any luck, Cass will starve."

The fae tried to smile, but his gaze kept drifting across the flames to where the Kreo were gathered on the other side of the camp. Katerina got the feeling that as long as he and Aidan had been sitting there, the vampire had been doing most of the talking.

She settled down beside them, taking a bite of meat before spitting it right back out.

"What *is* this?"

Even Dylan's infamous squirrel hadn't tasted so bad. As long as it had been cooked, it was like chewing on the sole of a boot. The flavor wasn't so different either.

Cassiel glanced over, while Aidan flashed a smile full of irony.

"Hyena."

She grimaced daintily, then returned the stick to the fire. "I liked them better when they were trying to rip my throat out."

There was a quiet chuckle as they were joined by a group of knights from the High Kingdom, the leader of whom was looking at Katerina with a mischievous smile.

"Rip *your* throat out?" he quipped mockingly. "I saw those flames of yours from over a thousand yards away. My guess is that nothing came close."

Her surprise relaxed in a smile as she pushed to her feet, giving him a quick embrace.

"Hey, Matti." It was easier to avoid the formalities when they were away from the castle. In the desert, they weren't a knight and a queen—they were just two people who'd played together since they were kids. "I'm glad you made it through."

Truth be told, she'd been too distracted by Henry Chambers and the constant question of Dylan to have even thought of him. She flushed guiltily and patted the place beside her on the sand.

"Please," he scoffed, flashing the others a good-natured grin. "It would take more than a pack of strays to do me in. I'm holding out for something really big. Go out with a bang."

Aidan flashed an obligatory smile, while Cassiel gave him a cold stare.

"We're in the Dunes...your wish might come true."

Distracted as he might be, the fae hadn't forgotten the first time he and the knight had been introduced. Nor had he forgotten Dylan's subsequent whining as to why he'd been forced to 'break bread' with a man Katerina had dated when she was sixteen. While the fae couldn't have cared less about the whims of a mortal heart, he felt a certain degree of loyalty with the ranger not present.

Matt froze for a moment, then forced another smile.

"Good thing we have this pyromaniac here to protect us." He gave Katerina a playful nudge, then gestured to the stick of meat smoking against the flames. "Are you finished eating that?"

She pressed it firmly into his hand. "Go for it. You'd be doing me a favor."

He took it gratefully as his friends drifted away, giving the others a cursory glance to make sure they weren't interested. Cassiel ignored him, while Aidan graciously shook his head.

It took a second to click.

"Of course," Matt said softly, staring at the vampire across the flames. "None for you."

Katerina shot him a quick look, but Aidan merely forced another smile.

"But thank you for the offer."

Much to her surprise, the perpetually-friendly knight didn't smile. He crossed his arms instead, giving the vampire an appraising stare while his charred dinner lay forgotten by the fire.

"I saw you fighting today," he said bluntly. "It was amazing. Truly amazing to watch."

A worthy compliment, but there wasn't a hint of a smile when he said it. Quite the contrary, the handsome man seemed almost angry. Staring across the flames with ice in his eyes.

Aidan looked up in surprise, watching him just as carefully. "Thank you." A look of unease flickered across his face as he made a quick gesture to the rest of the camp. "Everyone fought well—"

"But not like you," Matt interrupted, slowly leaning forward. "I've never seen anyone move like that. It was like...like smoke. You were there one second—gone the next."

This time, the tension was so great that even Cassiel stopped his silent vigil and turned back to the fire with the hint of a frown. Katerina had gone rigid as a board while Aidan straightened up slowly, draping his arms loosely across his knees.

He didn't speak. He simply waited. As if he knew the next line wasn't his.

"My first instinct was that it would have been good to have a few more of you fighting alongside us...*as was promised.*" Matt paused for effect, letting each word sink in. "But then it occurred to me that we'll see your kind soon enough. They just won't be fighting on our side."

A dead silence fell over the crackling fire.

The news hadn't been well received that the vampires weren't coming to the castle. It had gone over even worse when Katerina herself had flown low over the forest but saw no trace of their encampment in the trees. There were already in the badlands. Hiding, lurking in the shadows.

Awaiting the battle that was supposed to end all of their lives.

Even without the bond, she knew it was on Aidan's mind. He would grow quiet when no one was looking—those dark eyes scanning the endless sand. Somewhere, amidst those shadowy hills, his older brother was waiting. An army of darkness by his side.

"What would you have me do?" Aidan asked quietly. "Apologize?"

He had done so. Numerous times. It had made little difference, however. If it weren't for Petra standing tall by his side, there was a chance he would have been lynched by the angry crowd.

Matt leaned forward even farther, his eyes glittering in the fire. "I want you to answer a simple question. The leader of the vampires is your older brother, right? That's who's going to be standing against us?"

Aidan nodded stiffly, waiting for the other shoe to fall.

"Then my question is this: When the time comes...will you be able to kill him?"

Chapter 9

Katerina wasn't surprised when Aidan went out walking early the next morning. Nor was she surprised that any of the soldiers guarding the camp didn't stop him. It took a special kind of lunacy to confront a vampire. She'd been shocked when Matt had done it the night before.

Sleep hadn't come to any of them. Despite the exhaustion, despite the wounds. Cassiel was thinking about Tanya. Katerina was thinking about Dylan. And Aidan?

Aidan was thinking about all those people he'd sentenced to death.

"Hey."

The vampire spun around with a start—fangs bared, hands at the ready.

In any other moment, it would have been a victory. The young queen didn't know if she had ever surprised him. As it stood she approached with great caution, watching him all the while.

"I thought I might find you out here."

"You shouldn't sneak up on people," he retorted, still unnerved by the fact that she'd gotten so close. "Especially vampires. We don't react well when cornered."

Katerina pursed her lips to suppress a sigh.

He always did that. Whenever he was feeling guilty about something, he'd lump himself in with the rest of his kind. Despite their decades of separation, despite the fact that he'd dedicated himself to the other side. He'd done it before, when they'd met in the forest, slipping into harsh stereotypes he usually bent over backwards to avoid.

"Neither do teenage girls," she said lightly. "But you're always sneaking up on me."

He softened ever so slightly, then turned back to the horizon. Whether he was lost in thought or actually keeping watch, it was impossible to tell. She suspected it was a little of both.

"How did you even get past the guards—"

"What are you doing out here?" she asked directly, skipping right over whatever attempts he might make to deflect. "It's not safe for anyone to be out on their own."

He gave no reaction. His eyes never left the sand.

"It's probably safer for the rest of them if I keep a little distance," he finally answered. "I'm like a beacon otherwise—leading Merrick right to us."

Katerina froze in pure, unadulterated shock. "He took your..." She trailed off, unable to finish. Despite his other acts of barbarity, she never would have imagined it was true. "Merrick took your blood?"

Aidan nodded silently, staring off into the sand. "Many years ago. He took blood from the others as well. Didn't give them a choice. It's not like they would have said no," he added quickly. "But he didn't give them a choice."

Katerina stood there beside him, remembering with a shudder as the psychotic vampire told her as much at the feast—claiming a bond with Lysander, Diana, and even Aidan's own wife.

She had trouble saying the girl's name.

Finally, when the silence became too much, she shot him a tentative glance.

"He didn't give *you* a choice?"

Aidan hesitated, remembering a day he'd rather forget. "He didn't take it by force. Waited for me to come to him..."

His lips parted to say more, but he fell silent. Reading between the lines, Katerina sensed there wasn't much of a choice after all.

"I'm sorry about Matt," she said quietly. "He should never have said those things. I really don't know what got into him—"

"He was right," Aidan said simply. He was quiet for a moment, then gestured to the sleeping camp behind him. "We keep calling this the army of the five kingdoms, but it's really only four. I told the assembly the vampires were coming. I promised their aid—"

"You weren't lying, Aidan." Katerina circled around to stand in between him and the rolling dunes of sand—blocking them from sight. "They *were* coming. They just changed their mind halfway through. You know their fickle temperament better than anyone. You legitimately thought you could get them to come around—"

"Why do you always do that?" he interrupted quietly. "Try to absolve me from all blame."

"Because you refuse to do it yourself!" she cried. "Some things are your fault, Aidan. Some lives have been lost that you can never give back." She grabbed his hand, ignoring it when he tensed and pulled away. "But you've *saved* lives as well. Mine. Tanya's. Dylan's. Cassiel's. All those people back in camp owe you an enormous debt of gratitude for even attempting to make peace. I remember what it was like in Merrick's camp." She shivered. "They didn't know what they were asking..."

It was quiet for a long time. The stars fighting to be seen behind the desert haze faded. The shadowy sky began to show the faintest promise of pink.

"Your friend asked if I would kill my brother," Aidan said slowly, mulling over the question for the hundredth time. "The truth is—it doesn't matter if I would. I *can't* kill Merrick. You saw him back in the clearing. I couldn't do it even if I tried."

Katerina thought back to the moment in the forest, right before Kailas shifted into a dragon and they flew away to freedom. The two brothers had been locked in a deadly quarrel—one more blinding and vicious than anything she'd previously seen. But already within seconds, there had been a clear winner. Merrick was hundreds of years older than Aidan. There was simply no way to win.

"You don't know that," she said half-heartedly, remembering the way the vampire had caught Dylan with a single hand, ripping the face off one of his own people. "No one can win every fight, not even—"

"Merrick?" Aidan interrupted sarcastically. "Merrick could kill me in a second."

"But he wouldn't," Katerina replied with quiet certainty. "He-he cares about you."

She was going to add that he loved him. But she wasn't sure Merrick was capable of something like that. Then again, if the man *could* love, the person he'd love would be Aidan.

"You don't know what you're talking about," Aidan said coldly. "The man killed our parents right in front of me. I was six."

"But not you," Katerina insisted. "He didn't kill you."

Aidan threw up his hands in frustration. "Because he knew I'd never challenge him!"

"And what have you done every day since then?"

There was a sudden pause.

"...challenge him."

The queen's eyes glowed with triumph. "He hasn't killed you yet."

Aidan stared at her a moment, then turned back to the hills. "There's still time."

She left him there, alone with his thoughts, with all that dark uncertainty that refused to let him sleep. She was almost back to the encampment, when he called out quietly.

"Katerina."

She turned around and their eyes met.

"...would you have killed Kailas?"

Her lips parted, but she had no reply. The question had plagued her for longer than she cared to remember, following her all over the realm. She knew what she should say. She knew the answer he probably needed to hear. But in the end, she merely shrugged with a sad smile.

"I don't know."

BY THE TIME KATERINA got back to camp, people were already stirring. The morning patrol was coming to relieve those standing on watch, and the rest of the army was slowly starting to wake.

It wasn't often that she got to see these things, unobserved herself. Since arriving back at the castle, the queen had been under constant surveillance. Even during her pre-dawn chat with Aidan, she'd seen at least two knights and two Belarian wolves prowling along the sides.

But those guards had abandoned her the second she returned to camp, and with a detached sort of interest she watched a day in the life of an army begin to unfold.

The healers were always the busiest—flitting from person to person, never seeming to rest themselves. Thanks to Katerina's heavy-handed pour with Kailas outside the bear cave, the fairy tonic hadn't lasted long enough to treat everyone else's wounds. Amidst painful cries and the smoke of a hundred fires, the medics hurried back and forth. Rinsing bandages, easing fevers, coaxing bites of unwanted food. She'd often thought it was the most difficult job in the entire military. Even more so than the infantrymen who walked at the front of the line.

But the doctors weren't the only ones awake.

There was a sudden commotion at the edge of camp, and she lifted her eyes to see Tanya furiously pacing back and forth inside one of the open tents. A look of manic energy ceaselessly propelled her forward, and every now and then she'd throw up her hands mid-rant.

What she was saying, the queen didn't know. But her grandmother was listening quietly, nodding on occasion, having long since given up trying to speak herself.

Katerina watched them for a while before turning her attention elsewhere.

The knights of the High Kingdom were starting to wake—lots had been cast, and those still lying on sandy blankets were laughing good-naturedly at the ones selected to prepare the food. Matt was lying amongst them. The man was the son of a lord, the heir to a great estate, but he'd never let those things come between him and the rest of the men.

He lifted his head suddenly, as if he'd felt her staring. Their eyes met, and even so far away the queen could see him blush. He looked down a moment later, acting like he hadn't seen.

She continued her slow rotation.

Beside the remains of her own fire, Cassiel was still asleep. Aidan had returned and was sitting quietly beside him, staring at the embers and ash. With Tanya spending most her time with the Kreo, Katerina consumed entirely with Dylan, and Kailas and Serafina going off on their own, the vampire and the fae had found themselves most often left alone with each other.

It was a good mix.

Both were haunted by problems they couldn't possibly hope to fix, but both were equally determined not to let the others see. Protective to a fault, they had the same habit of shelving any inner conflict to deal with their friends' troubles instead.

As she watched, the fae began to stir. The vampire glanced down, then handed him a cup of something when he opened his eyes. Cassiel said something in reply and the two men laughed softly.

The higher the sun rose, the busier things became—partially because no one had any idea what might come sweeping over the horizon, and partially because dawn happened just as suddenly as dusk. No sooner had the sky lightened enough to see than a scorching heat came with it. Most of the fires were stamped out. Only those to be used for cooking were allowed to remain.

She watched as two grooms tried to coax awake a pair of stubborn horses. The blacksmiths were busy behind them, scarfing down bits of old stew and re-sharpening blades.

It was a truly fascinating sight. As deadly as it was practical, the army had all the makings of a self-sustaining little village. But amidst all the chaos and flurry...one person was standing still.

Michael.

The warriors of Talsing had camped along the edge of the perimeter, but their immortal leader wasn't with them. He was standing outside the camp entirely—up on a nearby bluff. He looked down as Katerina began climbing towards him, bracing himself at the same time.

He didn't need a blood bond to know what was on the girl's mind...

"Good morning." She decided to ease into it gently, flashing a charming smile. "Going to be hot again today, huh?"

His eyes twinkled with a genuine smile at her pathetic efforts, offering a helping hand as she neared the top of the bluff. "That's the thing about deserts...cold at night, hot in the day."

She nodded quickly, stifling a blush. "Yeah, I think I've heard that before."

The two of them stood for a while in silence, gazing down over the hill. In a strange way, it reminded Katerina of when they'd done the same thing back in the alpine sanctuary. The scenery couldn't have been more different, but she had the same person on her mind...

"Have you eaten yet?" she offered suddenly. "I could get you something—"

"Just say what's on your mind, child."

Dylan had told her once that he'd spent a significant amount of time wondering whether the immortal shifter could actually read minds. She supposed this didn't count as evidence one way or another. It's not like she was making it very hard to guess.

"We brought traders with us, to navigate the outer rim," she began tentatively. "But I was told that you and Petra could guide us once we get farther inside. You've been here before."

No, she wasn't making it hard to guess at all.

Michael bowed his head with a sigh, looking tired all of a sudden. Immortals were immune to the effects of time, but she could have sworn their time in the badlands had aged him.

But it wasn't the Dunes. He's looked like this ever since he found out about Dylan.

"One of the men mentioned something the other day," she continued hesitantly, watching his face for clues. "The Castle of Sorne. Have you heard of it?"

He looked directly at her and started shaking his head. "Katerina—"

"I saw Dylan there," she said in a rush, as if he might try to stop her. "Sitting by himself beneath a torch. There were loud noises coming from somewhere lower down... He was frightened."

If she was being honest, his expression had gone past frightened. Past angry, or hopeless, or resigned. It was something she'd never forget. Not for as long as she lived.

Michael sucked in a quick breath, then turned his face away deliberately.

"The Knight was manipulating you. Showing you whatever he wanted you to see—"

"It was real," Katerina insisted passionately. "I know it was real. Just like the hyenas he said were coming. Just like...just like when he offered to trade Dylan's life for the pendant."

Michael glanced back, his eyes enormous and hard to read.

She hadn't told anyone else that part yet, only her small circle of friends. But if there was anyone she'd trust with the information, it was Michael.

More than trusting him, maybe there was something he could actually do about it.

"I wouldn't give it to him," she volunteered quietly, before he could ask. "I wanted to, but I knew it wasn't what Dylan would want. Not when so many lives rely upon it."

Michael's eyes flickered to the ruby stone. He shook his head slowly.

"So much trouble for one little gem..." he murmured. "I wish sometimes that Petra had never found it. That she'd simply thrown it away."

...never found it?

Katerina stepped right in front of him, taking his hands.

"We could go there together. We could get him back."

Instead of pulling away, his hands tightened around hers sympathetically. But there was nothing to make her hope. Nothing but sadness and pity in his eyes.

"No, child. We could not."

"Of course we could," she said urgently, refusing to believe otherwise. "We could both shift and fly there right now. You're incredible, Michael—nothing could touch you! If that three-headed thing comes back, then I'll stay in the air and distract it while you go inside and get Dylan."

"I cannot save him," Michael replied simply.

Katerina dropped her hands in frustration, balling them into fists to stop the growing surge of fire. "Yes, you *can*! You and I could leave right now. We could bring him back here *right now*."

"Katerina, listen to me—"

"No, YOU listen!" she shouted. "He TRUSTS you! He TRUSTS you more than anyone in his entire LIFE! You have the ability to save him! You cannot just LEAVE him there to—"

"Do you think I haven't considered it?" Michael snapped, losing his temper for the first time. "You think it doesn't weigh heavy on my mind? I've known that boy since he was a child. Raised him as my own son. To think of him in such a place—"

He cut himself off, unable to say another word. But Katerina was absolutely riveted, realizing for the first time how the old generation had already left its mark on the new.

Michael had saved Dylan's life—taken him in and raised him. Jazper had bonded with him and left a host of scars. Petra had rescued Aidan from his demons and taught him to hope. Eliea's death had forever changed Cassiel. Nathaniel himself had placed Katerina in a position of supreme privilege, only to sit back and watch it crumble and fall.

They've been waiting for this day to happen. They've been grooming us all this time.

...that just made the betrayal all the greater.

"I cannot save him, Katerina," Michael repeated quietly.

Her eyes filled with bitter tears as she took a step away. "You won't even try."

"I would try a thousand times over if I thought it would make a difference. But even if I could take him away from the castle, it wouldn't do any good."

Because there's no longer anything of Dylan to save.

"So you're just...you're just giving up?!" she accused through tears, wiping her face furiously with the back of her hand. "Just like everyone else? You're giving up on him—"

"Listen to what I'm saying," Michael interrupted with a touch of impatience. He put both hands on her shoulders, staring deep into her eyes. "*I* cannot save him."

But the queen was no longer listening. Her eyes were fixed on something over his shoulder, a surge of darkness spreading over the land. It took her a second to realize it wasn't simply shadow, but monsters. Monsters of every shape and kind.

"On second thought, that rescue is going to have to wait..."

Chapter 10

Merrick was right...they stood *absolutely no chance.*

Every single thought vanished from Katerina's mind as she stood beside Michael on the sandy bluff, staring out at the army of nightmare creatures that had come to kill them.

They wouldn't have a difficult time.

Never had she seen such a vast array of horrors. It was worse than the horde that had assaulted the enchanted castle. It was worse than all of her darkest dreams combined.

They stood in a huge swarm in the middle of the sand, not organized into battalions like the royal army was. Kasi demons stood beside renegade goblins. Herds of giant manticores pawed restlessly at the sand. A group of dark warlocks was twirling balls of black fire on the tips of their fingers, like they were about to play a game. And a strange group of shadowy creatures the queen had never seen before hung along the edges of the field, like ghosts made of smoke.

And those were just the things that she'd seen before. There were many she had not.

Staggering mammoths, each as tall as a castle turret, had planted themselves at the back of the swarm. Their mouths were chained with cruel bits and archers rode atop their saddles, holding torches of blood-red flames. Each one of them could take out thirty people with a single step. Each one had been fitted with spiked armor to take out many more than that.

Packs of skeletal jackals panted in hungry anticipation alongside a cluster of ghouls carrying scythes. A pair of cave trolls fitted with serrated shields and helmets dragged their long clubs in the sand. Even from a distance, she heard the insectoid clicking of Ravren as they lifted their sightless eyes and sniffed the air. Several towering Shien stood quietly amongst the Kasi, their shadowy cloaks blowing even though there wasn't a hint of breeze.

The sight of them alone was enough to send her into an early grave. The eerie silence did nothing but add to that effect. But then Michael murmured the scariest thing of all.

"...where are the rest of them?"

Her heart thudded to an uneven stop. "The rest of them?"

She didn't see how it could possibly get worse, how there could possibly be any more. But she remembered Petra implying something similar back at the castle. That she and her brother had been alive much longer. Long enough to see not only creatures such as those, but the older, far deadlier creatures that had come before.

"These were brought to the Dunes," Michael murmured. "They did not come from this place. You will recognize those when you see them. They'll be hard to miss."

Katerina cast him one final petrified look, then turned her eyes back to the sand.

The rest of the royal encampment seemed to be having a reaction similar to hers. People had frozen in the middle of breakfast, forks half-raised to their mouths. The horses were straining against their reins, screaming in terror as they fought to get free.

Cassiel and Aidan had frozen side by side, stunned by the sudden arrival. Both looked pale but determined. One was still holding his morning coffee. It was replaced quickly with a sword. On the far edge of the encampment, Kailas and Serafina were swiftly making their way through the crowd. Tanya was approaching rapidly from the other side. All of them met together in the middle.

There was just one person missing.

Where is he?

Katerina strained on the tips of her toes, scanning the enemy horde with a hunger to rival their own. The second she got over the visceral

shock of it, she'd realized that the arrival of the Knight's army meant
the arrival of the Knight himself. And that meant—

"The Carpathians, the Dugan mercenaries, the vampires..." Michael
was still murmuring to himself, staring over the embankment with a
frown. "None of them are here."

But on at least one count he spoke too soon.

A whisper of excitement rippled through the demons as a final
group appeared on the horizon, drifting across the sand like shadow
and smoke. They took no notice of the horrifying monsters around
them, but made their way to the front of the horde with a natural ease.
Gazing across the sand with the same enchanting, feral smiles.

This time, Katerina needed no introduction. She knew several of
them by name. Her eyes found their faces as quickly as if she'd known
them her entire life.

There was Diana in the middle, regal as a queen, with a pair of sharp
fangs that stood in frightening contrast to the gentle curves of her face.
Lysander was standing tall beside her, just as lovely, with his dark hair
pulled back and a strangely serene expression on his face. Maven was
just a step behind. Graceful, even in stillness. Bewitching, even from
a distance. With waves of unkempt hair spilling down her back and a
foot angled in the sand, as if at any moment she might take flight.

...which just left one.

Merrick.

He looked as magnificent as she remembered, an angel of darkness
making his way across the sand. Like the rest of his kind he wasn't wearing any armor, just a black silk shirt, open at the neck, exactly the same
color as his haloed waves of hair. Scores of demons skittered out of his
path as he impatiently cut straight through the center, eyes glowing ra-
diantly in the sun.

Katerina instinctively froze still, remembering his promise to murder her on sight. But those eyes seemed to be searching for someone in
particular. Someone on the wrong side of the divide.

Before he could find him, there was a deafening screech from the heavens. A second later, the haze tore open as the three-headed dragon streaked down from the sky.

...seven hells.

There were several screams from the royal army. Michael stilled and Katerina's hair flew back from the force of its mighty wings. The earth itself trembled when it touched down, shaking men and demons alike, but the moment it landed two men leapt down to the sand.

Two men.

The queen's heart came to a sudden stop.

Dylan.

It was like Dylan had never left. Like he hadn't been stabbed with a cursed blade and carried away into the sky. He jumped off the creature with the same effortless grace she'd seen a thousand times before, giving it an absentminded pat on the neck as he followed after the Knight.

The Knight.

She supposed she should be paying him some small degree of attention. But for the life of her, she couldn't take her eyes off the vibrant young man standing by his side. The most she could do was shoot a quick glance at Cassiel, who was watching every detail without taking a breath.

"Good morning!" Nathaniel called out cheerfully, smiling as his gaze swept over the dwindling breakfast fires. "I see you started without us."

A ringing silence followed this remark.

No one could take their eyes off the dragon, and no one had any idea what to say. Under no circumstances had they expected to actually speak to the man before attempting to kill him, let alone exchange quips of morning banter while the King of Belaria stood by his side.

The two men walked forward in perfect unison, coming to a stop just a few steps away from Merrick. The vampire gave them a curt nod before returning his eyes to the encampment.

"Not a very warm reception," Nathaniel murmured. It was amazing how he managed to make his voice carry, even over so great a space. "I'd expected better."

"I told you," Dylan replied flatly. "No sense of humor."

At the sound of his voice, something splintered in Katerina's mind.

Without thinking, she threw herself forward—half-stumbling, half-running down the sandy bluff. People called out behind her, but she didn't hear a word. She'd made it almost all the way through the tents, when a hand shot out into the air in front of her. Yanking her right off her feet.

"Let go," she panted, straining to get free. "Let me go, I've got to—"

"Are you crazy?!" Matt hissed, pinning her tight to his side. "He'll kill you."

The commotion didn't go unnoticed.

Thousands of blood-red eyes shot their way, dilating with an instinctual predatory hunger as the Knight took a step closer—tilting his head with the hint of a frown.

"That's strange...I thought she was with you."

Dylan followed his gaze, seeing the fire-haired queen for the first time. "She was."

For a split second, the rest of the world fell away. It was just the two of them, staring at each other from across the sand. Then he lifted his shoulder in a dismissive shrug.

"That's what we call a rebound."

There was a tittering of laughter through the demonic ranks as the Knight gave him an indulgent smile. It set Katerina's teeth on edge. Even more so when he reached out and fondly ruffled the ranger's hair.

Just a hundred yards across the sand, the army of the five kingdoms still had no idea what to do. The enemy was within striking distance—at least for the archers. Should they be loading their weapons? Preparing to attack? Any aggressive move they made, the devilish creatures would surely charge. Should they grab their weapons anyway?

...and what of the king?

"But where are the rest of your friends?" the Knight asked suddenly, clapping his hands as if they were on the clock. "I would have thought they'd come forth to greet you."

They certainly wanted to. But they were having some problems of their own.

Tanya had made it only halfway through the tents before the rest of the Kreo had realized she was missing and a coven of witches rushed forth to drag her back. Both Kailas and Serafina were being held in similar positions by the fae, and it was Dylan's own army—the pack of Belarian shifters—who had imprisoned Aidan and Cassiel.

Even from a distance, Katerina could see both men straining against the guards. If it wasn't for the fact that a part of them was still in shock they would have broken through already.

The Knight's eyes swept over the campsite, missing nothing. "Let's draw them out, shall we?"

The air shimmered as he made a strange gesture with his hand. The second after that, Dylan dropped to his knees. The eerie quiet that had settled over the armies shattered as he let out a piercing scream. Both hands wrapped desperately around his throat. His forehead touched the sand.

"STOP!"

It was impossible to determine which of the friends had shouted. The second they heard the ranger's cry they all flew into action. Breaking free of their protectors. Do anything necessary to keep them back as they sprinted recklessly across the sand.

Cassiel got there first.

He'd smashed his head back into the man holding him, then streaked forward. Stopping only when a barbaric weapon swung out of nowhere, pressing the tip of a blade against his chest.

He glanced down in surprise, then lifted his eyes to the man holding it.

...and kept lifting.

At least nine feet tall with a bald head and impossible muscles bulging beneath his skin, he towered over everyone else around him. Streaks of ceremonial paint glowed against his dark skin. He curled his lips in a cruel smile—giving the weapon a playful twirl.

Cassiel flinched as it tore neatly through his shirt, slicing open the skin beneath. A spattering of blood fell onto the parched sand and the vampires leaned forward with a collective hiss.

"Careful," the Knight said with a chiding smile as the bodyguard melted back to his side. "I might have spared you back on the mountain, but I make no such promises for my pets."

Pets?

Katerina's eyes widened as she stared at the swarm of vampires. Every dilated eye was locked on the blood trickling down Cassiel's chest, the primal craving overpowering any rational thought.

Merrick gave no reaction. His entire body had gone rigid the second he saw Aidan's face.

The younger vampire had appeared just a second behind Cassiel—actually grabbing his cloak the second the barbed spear swung out of the sky. He stood beside him now without an ounce of fear, ignoring his brother entirely to focus on the ranger still cringing on the ground.

"There's two..." the Knight cocked his head playfully, as if he was counting. "Still a few more to go. Ah, yes—there they are."

The rest of the friends broke free at the same time, flying across the space between the two armies, only to come to a sudden stop at Cassiel and Aidan's side. Dylan was still panting, digging his fingers into the sand. Another quiet moan ripped out of him, and they stiffened at the same time.

Katerina took a step closer. Kailas pulled her back.

"Stop," she said quietly, unable to tear her eyes away. "We're here...please stop."

The Knight's eyes twinkled as he stared down at her before he made the same strange gesture with his hands. At once, the enchantment lifted. The torture stopped.

A moment later, Dylan rose to his feet as if nothing had happened.

"*Cio.*" Cassiel spoke the instant he was standing, murmuring quickly in his native tongue. "*Il deharin nos morhmont tegalin. Tos miel un racien—*"

"*Tos dehas li morte.*"

The fae looked up quickly as the Knight answered in his native tongue.

"You forget," he continued quietly, "I've spent centuries with your people. It was your own family who taught me the language of your kind."

Cassiel stepped back slowly as Dylan stared blankly across the sand.

"What did you do to him?" Katerina asked softly, checking the man she loved for further signs of harm. There were no visible signs of damage, but she couldn't get the frightened boy from the castle out of her head.

The Knight didn't answer. He merely smiled.

"I'm surprised you care."

With a particularly wicked expression, he circled his arm around Dylan's shoulder. Keeping his eyes on Katerina while he spoke into the ranger's ear. "I crept into her dreams. Gave your girl a choice between you and the pendant. She chose to keep it."

Dylan stared at Katerina for a long moment, then turned his away.

"Good." There was a faint hiss behind him and he glanced quickly at the Knight, like he was afraid he'd misspoke. "Makes for a better fight."

Why fight at all? Why not end this right now?

Without a hint of warning, Katerina threw up both hands—summoning that magical fire. There was no delay between action and thought. One second, they were standing there. The next, a wave of liquid flame was shooting across the sand, straight towards the Red Knight.

It should have killed him. It should have burned right through whatever was left of his shriveled heart. But then the strangest thing happened.

Dylan leapt in front.

There was a tortured cry as the ranger fell back to earth, absorbing the deadly attack meant for his captor. White-hot flames consumed his body, licking at every exposed inch of skin as he writhed and screamed on the desert sand.

Katerina sucked in a horrified breath. The armies on both sides were frozen in shock. Even the Knight looked vaguely surprised as his enchanted prisoner burned to death in front of him.

Only one person had the sense to move.

"Stand back."

Demons and men alike melted away as a tall man swept across the sand. He wasted no time in removing his cloak and throwing it over the fallen ranger. After some muffled cries and hasty patting, the thrashing stopped and a mangled body emerged.

Tears slipped down Katerina's cheeks as she half-collapsed into her brother's arms, but Michael never lost that eternal calm. With quick fingers, he pulled a tiny glass bottle from his shirt and unscrewed the cap—tilting back Dylan's head to pour the contents between his lips.

There was a moment where nothing happened. Then he gave a tiny cough and opened his eyes, staring with complete disorientation at the man kneeling above him.

"What—"

His eyes tightened suddenly as he looked down at his chest. The torn skin was already beginning to stitch itself back together, every trace of the burns melting away.

"Hush now," Michael soothed, reaching down to smooth locks of tangled hair away from his face. "You're all right, child. Just take a breath."

There was something deliberate about the way he said the words. As if he was quoting the exact script of something he'd said before. A strange expression passed over Dylan's face. His lips parted as his fingers tightened without thinking on Michael's hand. For a moment, it looked as though he'd like to join him. For a moment, it looked as though he was able to see the light.

Then the Knight's voice cracked out like a whip.

"Dylan, come."

The expression faded as the ranger abruptly released Michael's hand. A second later he was on his feet, quickly backing to the Knight's side.

"Interesting..." The Knight roughly looked him over for damage, pushing his head forward so his hair spilled into his eyes. "The enchantment is more powerful than I could have hoped..."

"Let the boy go."

Time seemed to stand still as everyone looked between Michael and the Knight.

The differences between them couldn't have been more pronounced. One had bedecked himself in riches and splendor, while the other was wearing simple clothes with sandals on his feet. One was armed to the teeth with an army of darkness by his side, while the other carried a single sword and had brought with him only those refugees who were strong enough to fight.

Yet despite all that contrasted them, there were striking similarities as well.

While both appeared to be in their mid-forties, there was an agelessness to them that you couldn't find in the mortal world. An ancient understanding carved into every line of their face. Immortality came with a degree of wisdom, but what these two had surpassed that. They had come from a time when the world was younger, wilder. They had seen things that the others had not.

"It's gotten to you, hasn't it?" the Knight said quietly, speaking to his old friend as if the rest of them weren't even there. "You look tired, almost ready for it." An almost nostalgic smile lifted the corners of his lips. "In a lot of ways, Eliea was the lucky one..."

"The boy," Michael repeated softly. "I want you to let the boy go."

At this the Knight flashed a grin, roughly pulling Dylan to his side.

"Why? Are you afraid I'm going to kill him?" In a flash, a blade was pressed to the ranger's neck—though you'd have never known it by his expressionless eyes. "After all that time you spent protecting him in your little monastery, all those years you taught him to look after himself."

The blade traced along Dylan's skin, leaving a thin trail of blood in its wake.

"It would be a shame to kill him now. Imagine how much longer you'd have to wait—"

"You always did talk too much."

There was a sudden commotion as Petra swept across the sandy wasteland, coming to a stop by Michael's side. Unlike her peaceful brother, the woman had embraced the path of a warrior. Twin swords hung down her back, and her twisted braids were laced with spikes of steel.

She glanced only once at the monstrous army before turning to the Knight in disgust.

"Do not mistake my brother's patience for providence, Nathaniel. Release the child or suffer the consequences." Her eyes glowed like heated glass, flashing with anticipation. "I'd love nothing more than to swat you and that foul beast you're riding right out of the sky."

For the first time, the Knight's smile faded. As his eyes swept between the siblings, a muscle in his face twitched. While he might be certain in the strength of his army, he didn't relish the prospect of facing the two of them together. Especially when his own immortal ally had yet to arrive. Looking through the demonic horde, there was no sign of Jazper and the Carpathians.

As he thought of Jazper, his eyes fell upon her counterpart.

"This must be the famous Aidan." He glanced between the two vampires before flashing the elder brother a wicked smile. "I can see the family resemblance."

Aidan straightened up slowly as Merrick made a compulsive movement with his mouth. It took Katerina a second to realize he was trying to control his fangs.

"I've never seen your brother beg for anything in his life, but he begged me for you. Was willing to give me just about anything I wanted...if it meant you could walk away free."

Aidan glanced between them in shock, but Merrick had gone very still.

"There's still time, young one." With a coaxing smile the Knight gestured over his shoulder, drawing the vampire's dark eyes. "Time for you to get on the winning side."

The army behind him was growing restless. Demons were chafing irritably against other demons. The vampires were still staring with unnerving attention at Cassiel's blood. There was a sound of creaking leather as the towering mammoths shifted uncomfortably beneath their riders, and the warlocks were sweating under their dark robes in the scorching desert sun.

The place was a powder keg about to blow.

Aidan took a measured look at the scene in front of him, then glanced at his brother for the first time. It was impossible to describe the look that passed between them. As long as she lived, Katerina would never understand it. Then he pulled in a deep breath and stepped back into the fold.

"Better to die right here than be someone else's pet."

The Knight's smile faltered as he pulled a heavy sword from his back.

"As you wish."

At those words several things happened at once.

The sword lifted high into the air as Aidan took a step back. But before the blow could fall, Merrick was standing between them. The handsome vampire cast a backwards glance at the Knight before turning to face his little brother. For a suspended moment, they locked eyes...

...then all hell broke loose.

The savage bodyguard's neck snapped over the hilt of his javelin as Merrick ripped the weapon from his hands. At the same time, he removed the notched blades. With deadly precision, his hand shot towards the demon horde. Ten knives flew from his fingers. A single perfect throw.

They flew across the sand...and buried themselves in the mammoths' eyes.

"*No.*"

The Knight actually forgot what he was doing, staring in open-mouthed dismay as the beasts let out a wailing scream and started rampaging across the desert. Blindly trampling everyone in their path. The entire army fell into disarray. Countless demons were crushed with every thundering step.

Their handlers tried hard to control them—pulling on the reins and shouting in languages Katerina didn't understand. But the beasts were inconsolable. Blood streamed down their armored faces as they flailed and thrashed, plowing through the demonic ranks.

The Knight turned back to Merrick, stunned to the spot. "What have you done?"

The vampire was breathing quickly, hand still outstretched from his throw. "...made a huge mistake."

The rest of the vampires froze perfectly still amongst the chaos, staring at their leader in shock. Then Lysander let out a rallying cry, and they turned as a single unit to rip apart the monsters standing beside them. Shrieks and screams echoed from the horde as they swarmed like smoke over the sand, wreaking devastating havoc as they tore through bodies—one after another.

There was no time for witty banter. No time for threats or good-byes. Dylan was still staring at the mammoths when the Knight grabbed him by the arm and started pulling him into the crowd.

"No!" Katerina screamed, lunging after them. "Dylan!"

He whipped around at the sound of her voice, but the demons were already closing in from every direction. He tried to catch his balance, but the Knight was dragging him across the sand.

Their eyes met for a single heartbreaking moment...then he vanished in the fray.

"NO!"

She screamed again, but the battle was already over. The demonic army was in full retreat as the Knight leapt onto his three-headed dragon and took to the sky.

He glanced down for only a moment, searching for Merrick in the crowd. Their eyes locked among the carnage, and in that moment the vampire sealed his fate.

Then he was gone.

IT WAS QUIET SOONER than was reasonably possible.

Considering how quickly the dark army had appeared, it vanished just as fast. One second, they were sprinting across the sand. The next, they'd vanished into the burning haze. Many people in the royal army had yet to pick up their weapons. Many had yet to set down their forks.

Only the vampires remained, standing uncertainly in the sand.

Their shirts were stained with blood and their fangs were fully extended. But even as that manic light cooled in their eyes, they started to look a little uncertain. They were vastly outnumbered with nowhere to run. They had come to kill the only people who suddenly remained.

Merrick was still frozen where he stood, as if the Knight's final gaze had rooted him to the spot. It wasn't until Aidan took a step forward that he whirled around—hands ready, fangs bared.

His brother froze immediately, hands lifted in the air.

"It's okay."

Merrick stared at him a moment before his eyes drifted to the army standing just behind. A silent weight descended upon him as he straightened out of his aggressive posture with a quiet sigh.

"No, it isn't."

The rest of the friends were in complete disarray. Katerina was still staring at the spot where Dylan had disappeared. But Aidan was literally breathless with relief. Not to have evaded his own death, but at the man who'd decided to save him. His eyes shone with actual tears as he took a step closer, trying not to smile. He gave up a second later and caught his brother in a fierce embrace.

Merrick stiffened in surprise, hands raised awkwardly above his brother's back. After a few seconds, when it became clear it wasn't going to stop, he lowered his voice to a murmur.

"I usually initiate the sinister hugs."

Aidan smiled even wider, arms clasped around his brother's neck. "Just go with it..."

Chapter 11

It was upheaval. Complete upheaval.

One would think that after that such a public display of allegiance, no one could doubt that the vampires had really switched sides—but it wasn't the case. The second the army got over the shock of seeing that three-headed dragon take off into the sky, they turned on each other. Then they turned on the vampires. Then they actually turned on their sovereigns for backing up the vampires.

...something their sovereigns were already hesitant to do.

"You're sure he can be trusted?"

Katerina asked the question for the hundredth time, standing with Aidan in the back of the council tent. Virtually every leader of the five kingdoms was currently stuffed inside, arguing at such a volume it would be a miracle if the sound didn't carry all the way back to the Knight.

"You're sure he's really switched sides?"

Aidan looked down at her, practically beaming in delight.

"Of course he has." His eyes glowed with happiness as they rested on his older brother, standing in the middle of the crowd. "You saw what he did back there. He saved us, Kat."

The queen studied him for a moment before following his gaze.

Strange as it sounded, she was inclined to believe him. The last time she'd seen the mercurial vampire, he'd vowed to choke the life right out of her. But she'd seen the way he'd looked at Aidan in those final moments. And she'd seen the look on the Knight's face as well.

Merrick had made a choice. And it was going to cost him.

It's costing him already...

Not since the assassinations at the peace summit had she seen such discourse and outrage rise up through the ranks. Half the people wanted to bow down and thank the vampires for their vital contribution, and the other half wanted to execute them on the spot.

While she was fairly certain Merrick would set fire to the tent before he let any harm come to his people, he looked unsure of his position at the same time.

As people shouted back and forth, he stood silently in the middle. Cataloguing every word that was said against him. Making a mental list of the offenders' faces in his mind.

"That's enough!" Abel Bishop shouted, raising his voice above the fray. "I don't care if they did march here against us, what the vampires did on the field of battle speaks for itself."

There were many voices in support of this. And many voices of dissent.

"He only did it to save his brother," Leonor argued, an ethereal delegation of fae standing by his side. "If Aidan Dorsett hadn't been standing with us, the vampires would still be in their ranks."

"But he *was* standing with you," Merrick said softly.

The tent fell silent as every head turned at the same time. It was the first thing he'd said since entering the camp and, given the nature of their argument, it was hardly a comfort. The fae elder stared coldly at the vampire, who returned his gaze with a look of perfect calm.

"Lucky for us," Leonor said sarcastically.

The vampire's lips curved up in a deadly smile. "Yes...lucky for you."

Sentiment and gratitude were quickly turning against him. It didn't help that he'd looked at the fae's neck before offering an angelic smile.

Katerina bit her lip, then pointedly nudged Aidan forward. "You should probably..."

He peeled himself off the wall. "Yeah, I got this."

With three graceful strides he crossed the length of the tent, coming to stand at his brother's side. He glanced over the people in opposition before resting his hand lightly on Merrick's shoulder—half to protect, half to restrain.

"I was under the impression that this conclave had entrusted one of the five kingdoms into the hands of the vampires—that they'd offered them a seat at the council. Has something changed?"

Several heated voices spoke up and he was quick to intervene.

"*Besides* the fact that my brother just saved all of your lives?"

Merrick's lips twitched in a smug smile as the councilmen floundered among themselves. They were still split down the middle, but luckily a strong voice was about to come to their aid.

"The vampires have done us a great service," Michael said softly, winding his way to the front of the room. "They deserve our gratitude, not our abuse."

He was the perfect person to have spoken, mostly because he belonged to no specific kingdom yet somehow seemed to command everyone's respect. Even Merrick's arrogant smirk faded as his gaze rested on the immortal shifter.

"Merrick," he called suddenly, eager to resolve this issue and move on to the next. "Do you pledge to fight with the rest of the five kingdoms against the army of the Red Knight?"

The vampire stared at him a moment, then nodded slowly. "Yes, I do."

Michael returned his gaze, those piercing eyes seeing through him to things the others could not. Then all at once, he nodded soundly. "That's enough for me. I suggest we move on."

"Move on?" Leonor exclaimed. "How can you expect my people to fight alongside his? To sleep in the same camp? There has already been trouble—"

The two men continued arguing with each other as Aidan discreetly pulled his brother out of the limelight—materializing them both back at the queen's side.

"I suggest we go outside," he said softly. "Nothing more we can do here."

Translation: Let's leave before my brother says something to incriminate himself.

Katerina stifled a smile and nodded, weaving her way through the crowd.

Sure enough, there was trouble in the camp. The vampires were assimilating as best they could, but their kind wasn't designed to play well with others. The hundreds of fae didn't help.

The trio watched as a woodland archer dropped off his bow and quiver with the blacksmith and started heading back to his tent—oblivious to the three vampires that had picked up on his trail. They followed him for a few paces before he turned around suddenly, freezing them in their tracks.

They stared at each other for a long moment, then the vampires melted into the crowd. The fae continued his journey, glancing over his shoulder every few steps.

"Will you speak to them?" Aidan asked softly.

"And tell them what?" Merrick answered under his breath. "That I've brought them to the middle of a wasteland, only to sentence them to death?"

Aidan looked at him quickly, but could think of nothing to say. It wasn't like his brother to be pessimistic—that wasn't what this was. He was simply telling the truth. He had seen the entirety of the Knight's army. He knew there was no way they could win.

Instead of searching for words to persuade him, Aidan went with another honest truth.

"Thank you for coming...it means a lot."

This time, it was Merrick who was incapable of speech. He stared in silence as his brother flashed him a hasty smile then disappeared among the tents, leaving him and Katerina alone.

She watched him for a few moments, then gave Merrick a tentative nudge. "Be careful. If I didn't know better, I'd say you were caring."

He flashed her a look, and for a split second she was reminded of his murderous promise the last time they'd met. A sudden chill ran up her spine and she was about to bolt in the opposition direction, when his eyes softened with the hint of a smile.

"Relax, princess. I would have done it by now."

She smiled shakily, but found herself in no way reassured. She was, however, desperately curious. An emotion she'd always found rather hard to keep to herself.

"You saw him back at the castle?" she blurted suddenly. When he glanced down at her, she felt obliged to add on the name. "Dylan?"

For the second time, he softened. Though this time he looked rather grim.

"You want to know if there's anything left of him—after being stabbed with that blade."

She sucked in a quick breath, almost too afraid to answer. "...yes."

The vampire paused for a moment, mind racing back through a list of horrors she would never know. Then he lifted his eyes to the camp with a shake of his head. "I don't know."

Not the answer she was hoping for. Not the answer she needed to hear.

"You must," she pressed urgently. "You must have seen something that would tell you, or have some experience with that kind of blade—"

"I saw him submit completely to the Knight's command," Merrick answered shortly. "Is that what you wanted to hear? I saw him lose any semblance of himself."

Katerina pulled back a step, her eyes stinging with tears.

"But there has to be a way to undo it," she finally managed. "If we kill the Knight, or maybe if we smash the blade—"

"You mortals are all the same," Merrick interrupted restlessly. "Searching for answers, when there are only questions."

"And you *immortals* are all the same," she snapped back through tears. "Answering in jackass riddles, when the people around you need help."

He stared at her for a moment, then offered another smile.

"I'm surprised he didn't take you. You were his namesake, after all. Not the shifter."

Again, the answer stopped the queen in her tracks. Mostly because it brought up a hundred more questions. There had been a moment on the battlefield—an exchange between Michael and Nathaniel—that she was at a complete loss to understand.

You look tired. You look almost ready for it.

A tiny line creased her brow as she played back every word.

It would be a shame to kill him now. Imagine how much longer you'd have to wait.

When the Knight had first appeared to them in the cave, he'd told them he'd been waiting for centuries in the shadows. Biding his time until the prophecy came to life anew.

Why would he wait? If he wanted the five kingdoms, why not take them unchallenged?

And how did it relate to the five friends?

While Michael had done everything in his power to keep Dylan alive, right down to jumping off the ledge after him when he tried to take his own life, the Knight had done all that he could to make sure that both she and Kailas would end up dead.

One protected his namesake at all costs. The other tried desperately to kill his own.

...why?

"I couldn't care less about your situation," Merrick concluded suddenly, raking back his dark hair. There were slight shadows under his eyes; she wondered the last time he'd eaten. "I'm here for Aidan, not to involve myself in your petty mortal squabbles. But Dylan is a lost cause."

She flinched as though he'd struck her, sucking in a quick breath. "You don't know that—"

"The man jumped in front of dragon fire," Merrick said flatly, ending the conversation.

This time, there was no mistaking the look on her face. It was as if the blade that had pierced Dylan had suddenly pierced her, too. Her blood chilled as her entire body began to tremble. If it weren't for a stubborn remnant of pride, she would have fainted right off her feet.

Merrick glanced down at her, hearing the change in pulse, then went abruptly still upon seeing the look on her face. For a moment he appeared to be thinking, trying to remember a script that had been forgotten long ago. Then he placed a hand on her shoulder, staring deep into her eyes.

"In truth, I'm sorry for it." His voice was almost gentle, as close as it could come. "I take no pleasure in seeing a man like that brought to his knees."

He left her a moment later. Standing by herself in the grass outside the council tent. Staring without blinking into the merciless desert sun...

THE REST OF THE FRIENDS had been whisked off in separate directions after the near-collision with the demonic army earlier that day. Their instinct was always to stay together, but since taking up the crowns of their respective kingdoms they found the decision was often beyond their control.

Kailas found himself immediately accosted with rhetoric and threats from the quarreling Knights of the High Kingdom. Serafina and Cassiel had their hands full trying to calm down the rest of the Fae. Tanya had vanished amongst the tents of the Kreo, whilst Katerina and Aidan had spent most of the morning pretending to be invisible in the back of the council tent.

It wasn't until a short while after Merrick left her that the queen wandered back to their old campfire—arriving just as the rest of her friends escaped there as well.

"That's it!" Tanya threw up her hands, sinking onto one of the large stones that had been dragged beside the fire. "I'm retiring."

"At least you're not immortal," Serafina answered with a caustic smile, settling down on the other side with her brother. "Cass and I are stuck doing this forever."

"Don't be silly, love." Kailas kissed the back of her hand, then stretched his long legs over the ground. "There's no way any of us will survive the coming battle. Forever won't last too long."

She laughed quietly as Cassiel gave him a long look. It seemed like the fae was about to say something cutting, but he leaned against the rock instead—looking utterly exhausted.

"I need to sleep."

"You need to get back to the council tent," Serafina chided quietly. "Leonor was looking for you earlier. He isn't pleased."

Cassiel shifted irritably against the rock, tilting back his head. "Leonor can wait a few hours."

It took Katerina a minute to realize she wasn't the only one watching. Aidan was staring at the fae as well, a strange expression on his face. He fidgeted uncomfortably, like it was difficult to breathe, then pushed suddenly to his feet—putting some distance between them.

"Can you-can you not do that?" Aidan stammered.

Cassiel opened his eyes, looking at him in surprise. "Do what?"

Instead of answering Aidan rifled around in a pack for a moment, then pulled out a spare bit of cloth. He wet it in the cooking water, then tossed it to the fae.

"Here," he gestured embarrassedly, "for the..."

Cassiel stared like he'd gone crazy, then lowered his eyes to the giant smear of blood painted across his bare chest. It had dried quickly in the desert sun. He'd completely forgotten it was there.

At once he squeezed the water from the cloth onto his skin, wiping away every last trace of the blood. The wound from the javelin wasn't deep and had already begun to close. To be safe, he tossed the cloth into the fire when he was finished. Then he slipped a new shirt on after that.

"I'm sorry," he apologized softly, letting down his long hair. "I'd for-gotten."

Aidan shook his head quickly, looking infinitely more apologetic than the fae.

The danger had passed, yet Cassiel was still curious. He'd seen the reaction from the other vampires when the Knight's bodyguard had pierced his skin—they were about two seconds away from forgetting the war entirely and ripping him to pieces.

Yet Aidan was standing right beside him. He travelled beside him every day, slept beside him every night. The two had spilled blood fight-ing alongside each other countless times before.

"Is it really that difficult for you?" he asked curiously, tilting his head to catch the vampire's eyes. "The way the others were speaking...is the temptation really that strong?"

Whether he was asking for himself or out of concern for his kin, it was impossible to tell. Probably a little of both. Aidan was quiet for a moment before he broke their shared gaze.

"Yes."

Cassiel took a while to absorb this, still staring at the vampire. His brow tightened and he appeared to be thinking very hard. Then slowly, *very* slowly, he offered out his wrist.

Katerina's mouth fell open, and Serafina let out a gasp.

"What are you doing?" Aidan asked in alarm. He stumbled back, sounding a little light-headed. "Cass, don't joke around with something like that—"

"I'm not joking. We're only as strong as the strength of our bond, right?" Cassiel's lips twitched with the hint of a grin. "Who am I to stand in the way of destiny?"

The vampire backed away quickly as Kailas stepped between them.

"You must be out of your mind," he said incredulously. "All those times I heard you rant against the vulgarity of blood-sharing. You were actually sorry when it happened to *me*."

"What happened to you was a tragic accident," Cassiel replied calmly. "What's happening now is a deliberate choice. You saw the size of that army; Michael tells me it's only part of the whole thing. We're going to need all the help we can get."

"This is different and you know it." Kailas stood squarely in between the two men, staring entreatingly into the fae's eyes. "Me, Katy, Dylan...we're all mortal. This bond will end for us in time...but you? There's a chance you and Aidan could be bonded for the rest of eternity."

Katerina was surprised at his insistence, that he was pressing the matter so hard. Thanks to Cassiel's everlasting hatred, he and the fae had a tenuous relationship at best. Perhaps it was just concern for Serafina that made him speak, but somehow the queen thought there was more to it.

Cassiel was just as surprised, but didn't let himself show it. Instead he stepped deliberately around the prince, pushing him back with his free hand.

"This isn't a full bond," he said softly. "And I understand the concept of eternity better than most." Their eyes met for a brief moment. "But thank you, Kailas."

Okay...what?!

"Cio." Serafina hovered uncertainly on the other side of the fire, looking like she was a just a moment away from covering her eyes. "...are you sure?"

They shared a quick look, then he flashed a winning smile.

"Of course I'm sure. Besides, you heard the prince. Forever isn't what it used to be."

Abruptly tired of waiting he closed the distance between him and Aidan, lifting his arm once more. Tanya made a compulsive movement behind them, but held her tongue.

Aidan's eyes dilated without permission as his fangs protruded into his lip. For a second, the impulse alone seemed to overwhelm him. Then he forced himself to look away.

"You don't understand...I won't be able to stop."

"Don't drink," Cassiel replied simply. "Just taste. That's all it takes, right? A taste?"

Yes, that's all it took. And a taste of the fae's blood was clearly something the vampire had fantasized about since the day they'd met. But now that the moment was upon them, he was frozen.

"Yes, but—"

"Good."

Without an ounce of hesitation, Cassiel offered his hand. There was still blood smeared along the inside of his palm from the rag shining brightly against his fair skin.

Aidan stared at him a moment longer, gave him a chance to change his mind, then he reached out and wrapped his fingers around the fae's wrist. His eyes closed involuntarily as he lifted it closer. His entire body contracted as he pulled in a deep breath—

"Wait a moment."

Perhaps the fae was nervous after all.

With breathtaking speed Cassiel whipped a dagger out of his cloak, pressing the tip to the vampire's chest. It dug in ever so slightly as he flashed a friendly smile.

"Go ahead."

Aidan didn't bite, didn't drink. He simply pressed his lips to the inside of the fae's hand, almost like a kiss. When he pulled back, there was blood on his mouth. He tasted it slowly.

For a moment, nothing happened. Then—

"Seven hells!"

His eyes shot open with a gasp, as if he'd grabbed onto lightning or surfaced from the bottom of a deep sea. A thousand different emotions flickered in his eyes as he stared around in childlike wonder, trying to catch his breath. One hand shot out for balance. The other reached instinctively for Cassiel—trying to pull him back for more.

But the fae had already retreated to a safe distance. Aidan had taken care to release his hand before tasting the blood. He was already on the other side of the fire.

"Maybe you should take off for a while," Katerina murmured, watching as Aidan blinked down at his own hands like he'd never seen them before. "Give him time to...collect himself."

Cassiel nodded quickly, looking a little out of sorts himself. Without wanting to draw further attention to himself, he swiftly left the clearing. Serafina went with him, just in case.

By the time Aidan noticed they were missing, they were already gone.

"Where did—" He glanced up just in time to see their white hair disappearing through the tents. "Yeah, that's-that's probably for the best."

His hands were coiled and trembling. One foot was bouncing in the sand. Those dark eyes had dilated past the point of any color and he had yet to retract his fangs.

Remembering with horrific detail the last time the vampire had lost control Kailas casually stepped forward, blocking the path the fae had taken from view. He probably should have changed the subject, but a part of him was just as incurably inquisitive as his sister.

"How did it taste?" he asked curiously.

It was the first time the two men had really spoken since forging a bond, but the vampire was too overwhelmed to notice. His body was staying grounded through force of will alone.

"...exactly how I imagined it would."

He took several deep breaths, trying to pull himself together. They were probably meant to soothe, but did nothing but hyperventilate him further as he flashed the prince his most polite smile.

"I would like very much to eat your friend. Would that be possible, please?"

Kailas grinned in spite of himself. "Yeah, I'll ask him."

A joking exchange, but his hand was on the hilt of his sword.

"Don't even ask him, just..." Aidan bit down on his lip with a grin, then let out a sudden cry. There was a sharp *crack* as the rock he'd kicked in frustration broke in two. "Sorry, I'm just going to..." He trailed off, running his hands through his hair. "I need-I need some fresh air."

...we're outside.

The twins shared a quick glance, but the vampire had already left. Weaving his way through the tents—in the same direction as the fae.

"Aidan," Kailas called sharply.

The vampire let out a sigh, then headed in the opposite direction.

Brother and sister watched him go until he was just a dark speck against the sand. The fae were on the far side of the encampment, with an entire army in between. When at last they were satisfied they sat back down beside the fire, staring pensively into the flames.

"How is it possible?" Kailas murmured. He lifted his head, catching his sister's eyes across the fire. "How is it possible that we're the most normal people here?"

She tried to smile, but ended up shaking her head.

"I can't believe Cassiel just did that."

There was a quiet rustling of fabric as Tanya wrapped her arms around her chest.

"He didn't do it for himself," she said grimly. "He did it for Dylan."

Chapter 12

For the next six hours, Merrick stood in front of the council and told them everything he'd seen in the Knight's camp. Covens and packs. Weapons and firepower. Overall numbers. He spoke quickly and succinctly, painting a clear picture whilst reserving judgement of his own. But this was one of those situations where impartiality didn't make a difference. The facts spoke for themselves.

For possibly everyone who'd travelled to the desert, the fight would be their last.

"Should we wait?" Bishop murmured, turning to share a look with a trio of fae. "Go back to the five kingdoms, try to assemble a larger force—"

"We've brought everyone we reasonably can," Atticus Gail interrupted. "Only woman and children are left. We should strike *now*—before the Knight has a chance to regroup."

While the man could usually be counted on as a level head, nearly all of that composure had vanished when he saw Dylan standing in the sand. The other shifters practically had to drag him off the battlefield. He'd been attempting to race after the retreating army on foot.

Bishop turned to him, a trace of pity in his eyes.

"You have lost reason when it comes to this," he said softly. "We must do what is best for the realm as a whole—"

"No, he's right," Merrick interrupted. It was the first time he'd offered an opinion of his own, and the tent instantly fell quiet. "The only reason the Knight came with half his forces was to scare you into waiting until the Carpathians arrived. If there's the slightest chance that hasn't happened, then we should march to the castle right now."

It felt strange to be taking advice from a vampire, but the logic was undeniable and a quiet murmur of assent followed his words. If there was a chance that their fight would be easier today than it would be to-morrow, they didn't have much of a choice.

"We can march for the castle today," Michael agreed. "Carry the wounded."

Bishop nodded slowly, then turned to Katerina. The other four kingdoms had already voiced their consent, but he would wait for the final order from his queen.

She hesitated a moment, then nodded.

"Then it is decided," he declared, pushing to his feet. "We go to war."

IN THE TWELVE-HOUR trek to get to the castle, Katerina discovered there was much more to fear about the Dunes than miles of scorching sand. Just a few hours in, the ground they were walking on collapsed in a giant sinkhole. Fifty men were killed. A few hours later, a swarm of what looked like locusts descended upon the weary soldiers, diving down from the sky and ripping away bits of skin.

By the time they made it to the shadowy mountains that separated them from the fields of Sorne, almost every soldier who had left for the badlands secretly wished that he'd stayed.

"Get some rest!" Petra commanded, raising her voice above the tired din of noise as the men went about setting up camp. "We attack at dawn."

A long silence followed after. There was simply nothing left to say. No more decisions to make or orders to give. The die had been cast—now they just needed to see where they landed.

For the first and possibly *last* night, the friends gathered together in peace.

"This is nice," Kailas murmured, leaning back to gaze at the dancing flames with Serafina lying in his arms. "Almost like old times."

It was quiet for a moment, then Katerina snorted under her breath.

"We've lost *all* concept of strange."

The others smiled in spite of themselves as they glanced around the camp. Yes, they had technically journeyed to a land of monsters. And yes, there was a very good chance those monsters were going to kill them before the following day was through. But in a way, Kailas was right.

It felt just like old times.

...with one person missing.

For the hundredth time Katerina lifted her eyes to the mountains, wondering if Dylan was looking back from the other side. He could surely see them from the castle. For the first time in what felt like years, the two of them would be sleeping under the same stars.

"We're going to get him back, Katerina," Cassiel said softly. "You have my word."

She tore her eyes away from the mountains long enough to flash him a sad smile. He was sitting with his back to a rock with Tanya curled up in his arms. Whatever trouble the two of them had been having, they seemed to have put it behind them for this final night. Their hands were always touching. Her head was always resting against his chest.

"You're awfully quiet," Katerina prompted, leaning down to catch the shifter's eyes.

It was wonderful to see her back with the rest of them, but Tanya wasn't usually the type to sit still before a big fight. Long, pensive hours staring at the fire weren't really her style.

She jerked out of her trance, returning the queen's questioning stare.

"Do you think maybe the pendant was leading you to the bear?"

Katerina straightened up with a start.

"...excuse me?"

The thoughtful mood shattered as the friends leaned forward at the same time, staring at the little shape-shifter with the same look of surprise.

"United by marriage, united by blood." Tanya chanted the line softly, her eyes locked on the fire. "What if *that's* what it was saying—that we need to make a blood bond. That's why the pendant led you into the forest. Not to find the wizard, but so you'd get attacked by the bear. Then you and Aidan would go off to meditate. And Dylan and Aidan would eventually be forced to bond."

The gang stared back in stunned silence, unable to think of a single thing to say. At first glance, it sounded crazy. But the longer they thought about it...

"You heard what the wizard said back in the cave," Tanya pressed quietly, looking at each of them in turn. "*Three are bonded—not good enough*. Maybe we all have to do it."

"Sera and I can't," Cassiel reminded her.

"Sera doesn't have to."

"But *I* can't," he insisted. "I did everything I could yesterday. A fae and a vampire cannot form a blood bond."

It was quiet for a minute, then Katerina lifted her eyes. "Has a fae ever tried?"

A second later, the gang was on their feet. Hearts were racing, eyes were bright and feverish as they gathered together around the flames. Their shadows stretched high up on the mountain as they took as step closer, staring into each other's eyes.

"Are you sure about this?" Cassiel said quietly, one hand wrapped protectively around his girlfriend. "With Dylan already gone, I'm not sure it even..."

But for the first time in what felt like ages, Tanya's eyes were sparkling with a hint of their old light. There was a moment as she stared up at Aidan that she seemed to be considering. Then, without a word of warning, she leapt up and bit him on the neck.

"What are you doing?!" he gasped, hand flying to his throat.

She clung on like a monkey, grinding her teeth against his skin. "...bonding..."

With a cry of pain and exasperation, he pried her loose—plopping her back down on her feet. Katerina looked down quickly to hide a grin, and Cassiel grimaced apologetically on her behalf.

"I couldn't get through," she fumed, staring up at his neck with great determination.

"Didn't stop you from trying!" Aidan shot back, looking scandalized. One hand was still raised protectively between them. "That's why we have *fangs*, you psychopath!"

"You're right." She pulled out her knife. "Let me try again—"

The tiny girl revved up for another jump but Cassiel caught her by the shoulders, holding her steady as Aidan swiftly bit open a vein in his wrist. At that point, all her momentum stalled.

She looked down, made a face, then shook her head. "I'm going to be sick."

"Tanya," Katerina chided gently.

Aidan fixed his eyes on mountains, muttering under his breath. "That's all right, it's only the most insulting thing she could possibly say..."

"Honey, you have to do this," Cassiel said gently. "We all agreed."

"I've changed my mind."

"I'll just keep standing here," Aidan said lightly. "Bleeding."

"It's *revolting*," she said again, crinkling her nose as his wrist trickled blood onto the sand. "I can't just put my mouth on his mangled skin and—"

"You don't have to drink it, Tan," Cassiel interrupted. "You just need a taste."

Moving with a strange grace, considering what he was doing, Cassiel swept a finger along the vampire's wrist before sliding it into her mouth. The others stared with wide eyes, then looked away at the same time. There was something bizarrely erotic about it. Not between Tanya and Aidan. But between Tanya and Cassiel. Her eyes blazed into his as she ran her tongue along his finger, licking the blood clean. When she was finished, she stretched up on her toes with a whisper.

"Your turn."

With the crimson stain still on her lips, he leaned down and kissed her. Sweeping back her hair in the same motion, tasting the blood for himself. Again, it was oddly erotic. Until—

"Seven hells!"

The fae's whole body convulsed, doubling over at the waist. His skin flashed pale white, and before he could stop himself he spat the blood into the sand—ridding his system of it.

"Nothing personal," Tanya joked lightly. "He does that every time we kiss."

"Cass," Serafina was trying very hard not to laugh, "you have to actually keep it down—"

"I *tried*," the fae snapped, wiping his mouth. "It's just—" His body convulsed again and he grabbed onto Kailas for balance. "—impossible."

The friends shared a quick look before turning to Aidan—who was watching with interest.

"It might be impossible," he admitted. "You remember what I said about a vampire and a fae not being able to share blood."

"But you drank *his* blood," Katerina insisted.

His face lit up at the memory.

"And I'd love to have some more." His eyes glittered as he stepped forward, patting the fae comfortingly on the back as he retched into the sand. "Might even strengthen our bond."

Katerina smiled darkly. "And I thought all it took was a taste."

Aidan's face lightened with a look of perfect innocence. "Let's find out—"

He reached once more for the fae but Cassiel shoved him hard in the opposite direction, straightening up with a shaky breath. He alone didn't seem to find their banter amusing. Quite the contrary, he flashed them each a bloodshot glare and pulled out his knife.

"It'd be a real shame if one of those monsters didn't get to kill you..."

Kailas chuckled, stepping in between them. He took the knife by the blade, but to Katerina's surprise he didn't sheathe it. He simply spun it around and nicked the fae's hand instead.

"What the hell are you doing?!" Cassiel demanded, jerking his hand back as a trickle of blood circled the inside of his wrist. "He wasn't being serious—he doesn't need more of mine!"

Aidan twiddled his thumbs, avoiding everyone's eyes. "Better safe than sorry..."

"You must have a death wish!"

There was a chance things could have escalated further but Katerina leapt forward, taking the knife from her brother's hand with a conspiratorial grin. They didn't need telepathy to read each other's minds. It was the same thing they'd done every summer since they were children.

"He doesn't need more of yours, and you can't drink his," Katerina said simply. With the same knife, she turned around and cut Aidan's hand in the same spot. When she was finished, she stepped back with a little smile. "...but maybe there's a way you can still share."

It took both men a second to understand what she was saying. Then they slowly met each other's eyes. While the vampire was interested, the fae was unsure.

"I-I don't know if that's a good idea." Without realizing it, he angled his hand protectively behind his back. "What if it kills me?"

Katerina tilted her head with a sardonic smile. "What if the Knight kills us all because you were unwilling to take this chance?"

Cassiel froze, staring at the vampire. "...I'd be okay with it."

Katerina laughed out loud, shoving him forward. "Come on, you coward. Quit stalling."

A few things to avoid in the supernatural world...

Don't gamble with goblins. Avoid trading recipes with a witch. And *never* call a fae a coward.

For a split second, it looked like Cassiel was about to decapitate the young queen right there on the spot. Instead, he strode forward and grabbed the vampire's hand.

From a distance, it must have looked utterly bizarre—as if they were merely shaking. But as the firelight danced up around them, a strange transformation began to take place.

Cassiel jerked away, then held on tighter—lips parting as he stared into the vampire's eyes. A little breeze stirred up around them where none had existed before, and when they finally managed to pull their hands away it took almost all their impossible strength just to do so.

"I've never..." Aidan took a second to catch his breath, shivering despite the heat of the fire. "I've never felt something like that before."

Cassiel froze where he was standing, eyes on the flames. "...neither have I."

Tanya was the last to complete the circle, pricking the tip of her finger with a dagger before smearing it messily across the vampire's hand. Aidan cast a strained look towards the heavens, as if it was a highly undignified way to go about such a thing, then licked it obligingly off his skin.

The same thing happened. The same subtle shift. The contrast between the two friends was incredible as they stared at each other, yet they were somehow the same.

"We should get some rest," Kailas said softly, watching them curiously even as he settled back into his bed. "Petra says we leave at sun-up. There is this death battle we need to attend."

The others nestled down beside him without saying a word, feeling abruptly tender towards each other without being willing to mention the reason why. Instead of scattering around the fire, they found them-selves lumped together on the same side. Huddling for warmth, even though the flames had them pleasantly heated. Heads resting together as their hands gradually entwined.

It was a striking image. One the fates had predicted long ago.

But again, someone was missing.

So again, Katerina was unable to sleep.

THE GROUP OF FRIENDS must have been truly exhausted from their travels, because none of them even stirred as Katerina got up and started walking away from the crackling fire. There were many oth-ers still blazing further in the camp. Insomnia wasn't at all uncommon among soldiers before a battle, and she got many a bowed head and qui-et salute as she passed by.

She wasn't looking for anything in particular. She didn't even see Merrick, until she'd almost walked right into him—standing by himself at the top of a sandy bluff.

"You again." He glanced down at her before turning away, hands in his pockets, staring up at the night sky. "What have I done to deserve a royal chaperone?"

What haven't you done?

Instead of asking the question out loud Katerina took the spot be-side him, flashing a sweet smile as she shivered slightly in the night breeze.

"Just making sure my new ally doesn't make a break for it," she said lightly. "I've heard from reliable sources that you never pick the losing side."

It wasn't wise to antagonize a vampire either, but Merrick only smiled. He seemed to have a generous sense of humor—up until the precise moment he did not.

"That's true." His smile faded slightly as his eyes swept over the camp. "But it seems this time that the losing side picked me."

They stood there a while without speaking. With most people the silence would have been oppressive, but Merrick wasn't like most people. To be honest, it was a trait that all the vampires Katerina had met seemed to share. The ability to exist in a world of perfect silence.

"What are you doing up here?" she finally asked. Given the level of trust for those of his kind, it was highly unlikely he'd been asked to keep watch.

"I *wasn't* looking for the fae," he replied quickly.

She glanced over in surprise. The thought hadn't occurred to her, but she made a mental note to give Serafina a head's up when she got back to camp.

"What are *you* doing here?" he asked playfully, turning to look at her straight on. "I thought you'd be sleeping off the magic of that blood bond, along with the rest of your friends."

She froze perfectly still, wondering again if the vampire could read minds.

"I can't read minds." He turned back to the sea of tents, looking over them slowly before his eyes came to rest on a particular one. "You think I can't tell when Aidan does something like that less than a hundred yards away? You forget, darling—I've tasted my brother's blood."

No, she hadn't forgotten. Nor had she forgotten the circumstances in which it happened.

"Are you angry with me for bonding with him?" she asked boldly. "Or are you angry because, *this* time, the bond was his choice?"

Merrick's eyes sparked, and she sensed she'd strayed onto dangerous ground. He turned to her slowly, looking down from a good six inches above.

"Listen carefully, little girl. I care not if my brother has welcomed you with open arms." He began walking down the hill. "Do not presume to know anything about me or my family."

It was a clear warning. Only a fool would have disobeyed. But ever since the circle had been completed by that final drop of blood, a strange sensation had come over her. Making her speak when she shouldn't, giving her a sense of abandon she quickly put to the test.

"I know you killed your parents."

Merrick froze where he stood, then slowly turned around. Despite the lack of moonlight, his eyes still seemed to glow in the dark. The two of them stared at each other for a moment, then he said the last thing in the world she'd expected him to say.

"I killed my parents, because they were going to kill my little brother."

EVEN IN HINDSIGHT, Katerina never understood how she got Merrick to tell the story.

No amount of intentional convincing could have ever swayed him, but the vampire was bored and distracted, and there was a decent chance the two of them were about to die.

Instead of killing her just for asking, instead of ripping out her throat and tossing it carelessly into the sand, the two of them sat down together. Arms on their knees. Staring out at the camp.

"When Aidan was a baby...I was enchanted by him."

The vampire spoke softly, his gaze a thousand miles away.

"The things he did, the noises he'd make, watching him discover things for the first time. I was enchanted by him, and he was enchanted by everything. Blades of grass, the rustling of wings, tiny specks of dust twinkling in the sun. Things I had long stopped noticing myself."

His face softened as he remembered, gentling with an expression she'd never seen.

"They delighted him, and he delighted me. I took him everywhere, like he was my personal property. When the camp moved from place to place, I carried him under my arm."

Those dark eyes sharpened with a sudden chill.

"The first time I heard my parents discuss it, we were sitting by a river. We were going to attack some neighboring clan, couldn't take a baby, and they didn't want to bother leaving someone behind to protect him. They decided to dispose of him instead."

The queen was shocked, but the vampire was thoughtful.

"It wasn't a difficult decision. They'd never wanted another child. One was risky enough."

"Why?" Katerina asked breathlessly, afraid to move an inch.

He glanced down with a smile she would never forget.

"We have a habit of killing our parents."

Oh. Right.

It was quiet for a moment, then the story continued.

"But my parents didn't want to be just another clan, they wanted to create a dynasty. The Dorsett dynasty. That's where I came in. Aidan...was pushing their luck."

He picked up a handful of sand, letting it trickle between his fingers. Katerina watched, absolutely mesmerized, until the final grain dropped.

"They debated tossing him into the river. He was small enough, he couldn't swim. I threw a tantrum. Killed two guards." He caught her look, but he brushed it off with a dismissive shrug. "I was young. And having met me, you'll find it easy to believe that tantrums weren't uncommon."

She wisely chose to keep her mouth shut.

"They decided to let him live—if only to placate me. The next time they tried, he was six. I knew there was no reasoning with them. Funny thing was, we were by that same river."

For a suspended moment, he stared off into space.

"I left Aidan on the shore and tore their hearts out," he finished abruptly.

Katerina's jaw went slack as the base of her skull started tingling. She wanted to get up and walk away, but she was suddenly feeling dizzy. It could have been the story. Or it could have been Merrick himself. The man had a way of taking hold of you, using nothing but his words.

"I'll never forget the look on his face," he murmured under his breath. "Those wide eyes, staring at me." He hesitated a moment. "I guess...I would have preferred he'd never seen."

The queen pulled in a deep breath—in through her nose, out through her mouth. When she was confident she could speak without her voice shaking, she turned to him in the dark.

"You should tell him that."

He glanced down suddenly, almost as if he'd forgotten she was there. "What?"

She blinked incredulously. "That you did it to save him. That it was the only way to save his life."

Merrick shook his head. "Why would I tell him that?"

She wanted to shake him. But she valued her life. "He thinks you're a homicidal monster!"

"He isn't wrong."

"He thinks you hate him."

There was a slight pause, then Merrick turned his eyes back to the camp.

"That's his mistake."

The conversation dropped without another word. The vampire returned to whatever he'd been thinking before she'd arrived; Katerina leaned back on her elbows, shaking her head.

I will NEVER understand men. Or vampires. Vampire men are the worst.

"Is this why Aidan bonded with you?" Merrick asked suddenly.

She looked up to see him staring at her with a handsome, curious smile.

"What do you mean?" she answered a little breathlessly. She would have given anything to stop the blush that followed. However, in his presence, that kind of thing simply couldn't be helped.

Merrick didn't notice. He must have grown impervious over time.

"You're pretty to look at, but you're also easy to talk to." He cocked his head to the side, putting it together for the first time. "In my experience, those things seldom go hand in hand."

She didn't know whether to feel complimented, or offended on behalf of all her kind.

"Aidan bonded with me to save my life," she answered a little stiffly. "I was attacked by a magical panther that mauled me and bit off most of my hand."

The vampire's expression never changed.

"Oh..." He nodded vaguely. "I've been in situations like that."

Somehow, the queen didn't doubt it.

They lapsed into silence for a while more. Both trying to draw out the night as long as possible. Neither one ready to lay down their heads and sleep. For the most part, the activity in the camp was winding down. But a sudden movement by one of the fires caught Katerina's eye.

A girl had emerged from one of the tents and was dipping a blade into the blacksmith's fire. The second it was hot enough, she lay it across a long table and started pounding it with all her strength. Completely oblivious to the deafening noise echoing around her. A pile of finished blades was already on the ground beside her. Katerina was surprised no one had asked her to stop.

A second later, she realized why.

"Lovely, isn't she?" Merrick said quietly.

Together they watched as Maven swung the heavy mallet again and again, sending up sprays of golden sparks every time it touched the blade.

"I thought she was going to kill me," Katerina whispered. "The last time we met."

"She *was* going to kill you," Merrick answered calmly, his eyes following every move of her slender arm as it flew through the air. "But you don't need to worry about that now."

Katerina shot him a strange look. Because he was offering to protect her? Because their people had pledged to fight on the same side? She turned back to the camp, looking grim.

"I'll need to speak with her afterwards," she murmured. "If we both make it through this battle, then everything will change."

"No, it won't."

She glanced at Merrick again, sure that she'd heard him incorrectly. But he was staring at Maven with that same expression, watching the glow of burning metal flicker across her face.

"What do you—"

"If anyone in the five kingdoms is still breathing when the sun finally sets, things will go back to exactly the way they were before," Merrick said impassively. "Your people will continue to despise mine. My people will continue killing yours. For food, for sport. The years will pass, and sooner or later we'll meet again on this same battlefield. We'll just be standing on different sides."

The words weren't said with any threat or malice, but they chilled the queen, nonetheless. In his voice, she heard more than a promise. There was a history of things she would never understand.

Centuries of mistrust and slaughter. Mobs with pitchforks and rigid courtrooms. Villagers snatched into dark alleys. People with pale, beautiful faces burned to death at the stake.

A white flag stood above it all. Raised for the love one man bore his brother. But it would soon be lost once again. Buried in a never-ending cycle of vengeance and blood.

She and Merrick sat there together, watching side by side. Friends today. Enemies tomorrow.

It was quiet for a few minutes, then she twisted her head and gave the vampire the hint of a smile. "Until that day."

His eyes glowed as the smile was returned. "Until that day."

With those parting words he pushed to his feet and headed off into the night, striding down across the sand to where the vampires had made camp on the far side of the embankment.

He was halfway there, when he turned around suddenly, catching Katerina's eye.

"And you were wrong again, sweetheart."

She looked up in surprise, arms wrapped around her chest. "About what?"

In the distance, they heard the violent crash of the hammer.

"Maven has no intention of surviving this fight."

Chapter 13

In the days leading up to the final battle, when Katerina had been walking across stretches of endless desert, she couldn't help but imagine all the horrific monsters waiting for her on the other side. It probably wasn't the wisest use of her time, but a part of her couldn't help it.

She found herself thinking of twisted manticores, skeletal cadavers, demons with fangs as long as her arm. With every step she imagined scores of Ravren, cave trolls and Kasi, that ferocious three-headed dragon dropping out of the sky to scorch her to a crisp.

Yet somehow she found herself facing something infinitely more terrifying.

Maven holding a blade.

The girl had her back to the queen as Katerina approached, bent over the shimmering coals as she roasted another weapon. But there were few things that could sneak up on a vampire. No sooner had Katerina opened her mouth to speak than a quiet voice drifted up from the fire.

"Coming to speak with me all by yourself? That's either very brave or very foolish." Maven set down the blade and turned around. "Would you like to guess which one?"

Every instinct was screaming to turn and run, but Katerina held her ground. As the fire wavered she actually took a step closer, reaching down with a stick to stoke the dwindling flames.

"Merrick told me what you were going to do," she said softly.

Maven tilted her head to the side, an animalistic gesture that made her look like some kind of feral angel examining the queen curiously in the glowing light.

"And what's that?"

Katerina braced herself with a breath. If she was standing on thin ice with Merrick, it was nothing compared to the wraithlike vampire with the wild eyes.

He chose to ignore the rules. In Maven's mind, they simply didn't exist.

"I'm sorry about what happened between you and Aidan," she said quietly, seeing the way the girl's entire body froze upon hearing his name. "And I'm sorry the two of us bonded. Please believe me when I say that it wasn't intentional—"

"Katerina," the girl interrupted smoothly, "on the battlefield, I can kill you and make it look like an accident. It would be more difficult to do it here, but I'm willing to try—"

"You *cannot* kill yourself."

The girl arched an eyebrow in genuine surprise.

"You think I...*that's* what he said?" Her eyes drifted to the exact place on the hill where Merrick had been standing, before returning with the hint of a smile. "Why would it trouble you?"

"It wouldn't," Katerina admitted. "To be honest, I'd sleep easier at night." She paused, and said each word with measured care. "But it would *destroy* Aidan."

Maven's eyes flashed, though her voice was icy calm. "*Aidan* left me." She began slowly circling the fire, eyes on the queen. "*Aidan* pledged to be mine forever, then refused to perform the simple ritual that would make it eternally so. The same ritual he performed in a spontaneous moment to save your life."

They were close now. Dangerously close. Katerina could see every fleck of silver around the dark irises of her eyes. She sucked in a silent breath as the vampire got closer still.

"I've known him for centuries," she continued, her voice low. "We travelled the world together, decided to marry, shared the darkest secrets of our hearts. You, little girl, have known him less than a year."

Maven came to a sudden stop, staring into Katerina's eyes. "So tell me again how destroyed he'd be, if I were to stop breathing."

It was in that moment the queen realized something very important. More than being dangerous, or beautiful, or too wild to touch—the girl was sad. Impossibly, incurably sad.

Perhaps she'd been that way for a long time. Perhaps Aidan was the only thing that had made it better. Perhaps seeing him again that night in the forest had finally broken her heart.

"Merrick can speech-make all he likes. If you're still here in ten seconds, I'm going to drown that pretty face of yours in the blacksmith's kiln."

...or maybe she never had a heart to begin with.

DAWN CAME QUICKLY. A lot more quickly than anyone would have liked.

Katerina felt as though she'd only just laid down, when the shadows suddenly parted and the morning sun burst through. It quickly burned away any remaining clouds, beating down into the camp with an almost human defiance, rousing the restless soldiers from their sleep.

"I don't understand this," Kailas muttered, wiping his forehead as he squinted sleepily into the sky. "How can even demons live here?"

"Most creatures of the Dunes thrive on heat," Serafina answered, pulling her long hair into a swift braid. "It's only fire that kills them. That's where you come in."

She gave her boyfriend a little wink, which he returned with a tired smile. Aidan was still sleeping but Katerina looked around in alarm, seeing two empty spaces beside the fire.

"Where's Tanya and Cassiel?"

No sooner had she asked than she heard the sound of raised voices from somewhere across the sand. The gang leapt to their feet at the same time, drawing their weapons as they raced around the jagged base of the mountain. If the Knight's army had decided to jump-start things themselves, they'd picked a bad group of people to engage. Fresh off a blood bond, the friends' usual protective nature had jumped at least a thousand degrees. They would tear the creatures limb from limb—

But when they rounded the corner, they screeched to a stop. There was a fight happening, all right. But it didn't involve any monsters. And on second thought, they didn't want to get involved.

"Just tell me what you were doing!" Cassiel demanded, holding out his hand.

Tanya was standing a few feet away from him, clutching something behind her back.

"It's none of your business!" she snapped.

"None of my..." The fae threw up his hands, cursing the gods for allowing him to fall so completely in love with such an exasperating girl. "You're my girlfriend! My best friend has been recently possessed, we're on the brink of war with a demonic army, and then I wake up to see my girlfriend sneaking around—"

"Fine. Then I'm not your girlfriend anymore!" she shouted. "We're broken up!"

Considering no one had ever broken up with him before, Cassiel took it well. He stepped back in surprise, swallowed back his first three replies then stormed forward, grabbing whatever she was hiding right out of her hands.

"Fine. Then I don't have any problem doing...this..."

He trailed off suddenly, looking down at the tiny glass vial. Tanya's face was flushed and miserable, but the fae was simply confused. Katerina grabbed Aidan's shoulder, hoisting herself higher so she could see. It was a fairy tonic. But wasn't that the one for...?

"Why were you going to drink this?" Cassiel asked incredulously. It was clearly an attempt he'd interrupted just moments before. "What were you trying to forget?"

He took one look at her face, then went deathly still.

"*...who* were you trying to forget?"

Tanya closed her eyes as a single tear slipped down her face.

"You."

The friends edged back the way they'd come, desperately sorry to have intruded, but Cassiel was simply stunned. He tried several times to speak, then shook his head in a helpless sort of way.

"...why?"

The shape-shifter mumbled something under her breath. Something so quiet, even the fae couldn't hear. He took a step closer, numb from head to toe.

"What did you—"

"Because I'm pregnant, you stupid dumbass fairy!"

Talk about whiplash.

At first, Cassiel just stood there—like someone had placed him on pause. Then his head jerked to the side and his lips parted in confusion. When he glanced at her belly, that confusion tripled and he took a giant step back. A sheen of sweat had broken across his forehead and he looked about ready to faint. Until all at once he began to smile.

It was unlike anything Katerina had ever seen. Never had she understood what it truly meant to be immortal until that very moment, because the look on Cassiel's face couldn't have come from any place like this. It was beyond anything she could have imagined.

Pure, incandescent happiness.

But whether or not Tanya had gone through a similar series of reactions, she had settled on something grim. And as it turned out, that eternal happiness was part of the problem.

"I'm pregnant," she said again, "with an *immortal's* child. A child who's going to age past his father in twenty years, grow old, and die. Just like I will..." Her eyes spilled over, but she forced herself to finish. "...while you stay like this."

It was a heartbreak fit to rival any happiness, but the fae wasn't having it. In a flash he crossed the space between them, reaching down to take both her hands.

"You have made me so *unbelievably* happy," he murmured, tenderly bringing each set of knuckles to his lips. "I can never tell you how—"

"It's doesn't matter," she pulled away stiffly. "We're broken up."

He shook his head, still wearing that beaming smile. "You can't just say no—"

"I just did."

He smiled again, reaching once more for her hands. "Tell me you don't love me...and you'll never hear from me again." His face turned serious.

There was a beat of silence, then she lifted her chin.

"I don't love you."

But Tanya had forgotten something very important. You can never lie to a fae.

A slow smile crept up the side of Cassiel's face as he stared down at her. A moment later, he scooped her into his arms—spinning her around and around before setting her down suddenly to place a hand on her stomach. His entire body thrilled to life as he knelt to the ground and kissed it.

"I love you, too," he whispered, pressing his forehead to her chest.

There were few hearts so cold they wouldn't melt, and Tanya's wasn't one of them. All the days of resolve she'd been building since waking up in the castle and discovering her situation crumbled to the ground. And she sank right down beside him and wrapped her arms around his neck.

There was some crying. There was some kissing.

Then all at once, Cassiel went dangerously pale.

"But the baby..." He pulled them both to their feet, turning to Aidan with a look of pure terror. "She drank your blood. Does that mean—"

"He didn't bond with the baby," Tanya assured him, unable to stop beaming now that she was finally able to say the word out loud. "I talked with my grandmother about it before I suggested the bond. She's been helping me through things...since I found out."

And on THAT note...

"Why didn't you tell me?" Katerina asked in a whisper, hugging her tight. She'd been unable to pry her away from Cassiel when the friends surged forward, but they were embracing, nonetheless.

"Tell you that Cass and I were going to have a baby...right after you lost Dylan?" Tanya shook her head, a look of fierce determination blazing in her eyes. "I didn't plant to tell you. At least, not until we got him back."

Serafina was bouncing on her toes, hands clasped over her mouth as she circled a slender arm around her brother. A steady stream of excited chatter was coming out of her mouth, so fast that her lips were a fluttering blur. Cassiel nodded on occasion, unable to stop grinning himself, but glanced suddenly over her shoulder to where the prince was standing awkwardly to the side.

"It occurs to me that I never apologized," he said abruptly. "For mistreating you."

Kailas froze where he stood, genuinely unsure what to say. "You...you had every right," he finally stammered. "There were a hundred reasons—"

"There were a hundred reasons," Cassiel agreed, dismissing each one in turn, "for why I *mistreated* you." Their eyes met in a moment of truce. "I'm sorry, Kailas. I truly am."

Whether he said it because they were standing on the eve of battle or because he'd just found out he was going to be a father—the rest of them would never know. The prince thought it had to be some kind of joke, checking discreetly to see if he was carrying a blade.

"You really don't have to—"

"You're a good man, Kailas." Cassiel gave his girlfriend another squeeze before flashing a quick smile at Serafina. "I'd be honored for someone like you to date my sister."

Excuse me?!

By now, Katerina was checking for a blade herself. But a strange expression settled over the prince. He paused a moment, then looked directly at the fae for the first time.

"...to date?" He cocked his head with a coaxing smile, obviously having something else in mind.

Aidan looked away to hide his smile, while Katerina rolled her eyes. It was one of the things she loved and hated most about her twin. He never knew when to quit.

"From a distance," Cassiel clarified. "I thought perhaps the two of you might send letters back and forth for the next few decades."

Kailas nodded slowly, fighting back a grin.

"A few decades, huh? And if I should die of old age in the meantime?"

The fae shrugged, as if such things couldn't be helped.

"Sera has lovely penmanship. You'd have some beautiful mementoes." He flashed a winning smile, resisting the urge to say, *We'd place them on your grave.*

Kailas nodded again before lifting his eyes once more. "...and if I had it in mind to propose?"

The girls lit up at the same time, while every hint of a smile faded from Cassiel's face. It was replaced with something rather frightening as he and Kailas locked eyes.

"I would bury you in a shallow grave."

He stormed away without another word, taking his girlfriend with him.

The others stared after them, completely overwhelmed by the series of events that had just happened—none more so than Kailas himself.

He glanced at Serafina, cheeks flaming with a blush, then Katerina clapped him encouragingly on the shoulder.

"That's progress."

THERE WAS NOTHING TO pack; the tents and everything inside them were left behind. It was convenient but chilling at the same time. If they won, the entire camp would be waiting exactly where they left it. If they lost... they wouldn't be coming back at all.

Katerina was nervously standing a little bit away from the rest of the army, waiting for the infantrymen and cavalry to fall in line. A sword was twirling quickly in her hand, but she hoped for everyone's sake that she wouldn't have to use it.

After she expressed a preference for fae blades, Cassiel had a sword specially commissioned and surprised her with it before the peace summit. It was spun silver. Not too heavy, not too light. A deadly weapon that felt perfectly balanced in her hand.

Of course, it had been lost when the castle was attacked.

The weapon she was holding now was a gift from Abel Bishop. She'd been too touched by the presentation to consider refusing, but the sword felt awkward and heavy in her hand. She almost dropped it halfway through a spin and glanced around quickly to see if anyone was watching.

To her dismay, someone *was* watching. But he was doing so with a smile.

"Not exactly what you're used to?" Atticus detached himself from a group of shifters, and slowly walked towards her through the sand. "Dylan told me you favor a fae blade."

"Oh. Right." Her cheeks flamed with embarrassment, but even more so at the sudden mention of his name. All morning long she'd been staring up at the mountains, knowing he was on the other side.

"It was a shock to see him like that," Atticus continued suddenly. "Before he landed, I'd felt sure that he...but no matter." He cut himself off quickly, reaching to the leather sheath handing from his back. "I wanted you to have this."

Katerina reached out automatically, then paled in surprise.

It was Dylan's sword. Not the new one he'd received at his coronation. But the trusted blade he'd carried around as a ranger. The one that had never let him down.

She lifted her eyes to Atticus, staring in shock.

"But how did you...?"

"I took it with me when we left the castle," he said quietly. "Was hoping I'd have a chance to give it to him myself. But...but I think you should be the one to do it."

Her fingers closed slowly over the faithful blade. How many times had she seen Dylan holding it? How many times had he used it to save her life? A rush of feeling swept over her as she lifted her eyes to Atticus with a tearful smile. She knew how much it meant for him to bring it all the way to the desert. She knew how much it meant for him to trust her with it now.

"Thank you." She gave it a tentative spin, pleased when it came back around. "I'll put it straight into his hands. He won't want me damaging it."

Atticus chuckled, backing away slowly. "Give him my regards."

He vanished a moment later, leaving her alone with her thoughts.

It felt nice to have some tangible piece of Dylan. She realized, with a sudden jolt, that if he didn't survive the battle the sword would be all she had left. His room in the High Kingdom had been sacked when the demons invaded the castle, and everything else he'd either left behind in the mountains or taken with him to the Dunes.

I could always go back to Belaria. Ask if I could have a keepsake to—

"Stop it!"

She said the words out loud, commanding herself to go no further. She would not allow herself to think of a life without him. She would not permit herself to consider a world where he didn't. He would survive the battle. And he would break free of the curse.

There was simply no other alternative.

"I can see I've come at an interesting time." The queen whirled around to see Petra standing behind her, arms folded with a smile across her face. "Don't mind me—I'd hate to interrupt."

Katerina flushed, and quickly hung the sword by her side. "Sorry, I was just...talking to myself."

The towering general came to stand beside her, staring out over the sand.

"I do that sometimes," she admitted without an ounce of shame. "I tend to find that the advice I crave is most often my own."

Katerina shot her a sideways glance, then stifled a grin. It was a very *Petra* thing to say. But the immortal warrior had come for a very different purpose.

"So the five of you have bonded." She caught the queen's look of surprise and cocked her head back towards the camp. "Aidan told me."

Katerina followed her gaze before returning her troubled eyes to the mountains.

"The *four* of us," she corrected. "Dylan's gone, and it's not like..." Her voice trailed off with a sudden sigh. "It's not like we came close to fulfilling the prophecy anyway."

Petra turned to her shrewdly, not a single detail escaping those sharp eyes.

"Explain."

Katerina threw up her hands, suddenly overcome by the hopelessness of it all.

"We're not married. We're missing a member. And-and I'm not even qualified to represent the kingdom of men. I'm a shifter. I could never have fulfilled the prophecy."

Petra waited until the outburst had quieted, then stepped into her line of sight. "You're not a shifter."

Katerina blinked up at her, wondering if she was all right. "Have you not seen the giant dragon that appears when I—"

"That doesn't make you a shifter," Petra interrupted. "It doesn't make you a shifter any more than your brother. Or your mother before you."

There was a moment of silence, then she actually had to laugh at the look on the queen's face. With cool fingers, she reached down and pulled the pendant from the front of her dress.

"Did you know that when I found this, I had no idea what it was?" she asked softly, staring at the ruby with faraway eyes. "I was tracking down a group of renegade shifters, climbing the peak of Mount Grace, when suddenly I reached for the ledge above me and found the ruby in my hand."

Katerina stared at her in silence, unable to move.

"Gemstones like that don't appear out of nowhere," Petra continued, "and this one was clearly more than what it seemed. I took it to a witch with whom I'd become acquainted, hoping for some answers. She left me with quite a bit more than that."

The general spoke slowly. She'd only told the story once before, confiding it in secret to her brother. Just that one time. Since then, hundreds of years had gone by.

"The second I entered her cabin, the witch—Evianna—fell to her knees in a kind of trance. Before I could help her to her feet she started to sway back and forth, speaking in a voice I'd never heard before. The words didn't make sense, but they imprinted forever in my mind...

Five kingdoms to stand through the flood
United by marriage, united by blood
Protected through grace, as only one can
To take up the crown, either woman or man

"When she got to her feet, she had no memory of what had happened. I tried bringing it back to her, even handed her the stone. And that's when she said something strange."

Katerina blinked in astonishment.

THAT'S when she said something strange?

"She said that the stone was only one half of a whole. A setting for a powerful crown. She said it was taken from the very heart of the earth—the fires beneath Mount Grace—and was destined to transform the wearer and endow him or her with great power."

Petra tilted her head as she stared towards the mountains, lost in a different time.

"Naturally, I had some questions. Magical objects aren't to be taken lightly, and I must have found it for a reason. I asked what she meant about 'transforming the wearer'. I asked about the great power it was meant to bestow."

"And what did she say?" Katerina asked breathlessly.

Petra broke free of her trance, gazing down at her with the hint of a smile. "She said only that the one destined to wear the crown must have the heart of a dragon, as pure as the fire from which the stone was forged. Only that person could wield its awesome might."

The queen lowered her eyes slowly, staring at the sand. Ever since discovering the prophecy hidden in the wall, she'd wondered why she'd been the one to find it. Why she and her friends had been singled out by destiny, but only four of them seemed to fit. Deep down there had been a nagging feeling in the pit of her stomach, wondering if the fates had made some sort of mistake.

But this proved it—the heart of a dragon.

"You are not a shifter, Katerina." Petra's eyes blazed as the words sharpened with an accent that had been lost over centuries of time. "You are a queen of men. It is up to *you* to unite the crown and the stone. That must be your only mission. If you should fail, we are truly lost."

IT WAS HARDLY A PEP-talk, but it was the best Katerina was going to get.

By the time the others joined her at the front, she'd hidden it firmly in the furthest corner of her mind. No need to add to their own troubles by telling hers. If she was truly the one meant to unite the stone and the crown, so be it. She'd just have to find a way to see it through.

"Are you ready for this?" Kailas asked softly, coming to stand by her side. He was fidgeting slightly in his armor, bending it at the sleeves. "Either the demons will get us, or this heat will."

Katerina stared up at him for a moment, then without a word of warning she threw her arms around his neck. The prince tensed in surprise but caught her, awkwardly patting her back.

"It's going to be all right, Katy," he soothed, smoothing down her long hair. "Just stay beside me, and I'll make sure—"

"Cass was right," she whispered. "You're a good man, you know that?"

The heart of a dragon, as pure as the fire in which the stone was forged.

Her twin might have his doubts, echoes of that dark enchantment might always weigh heavy on his mind, but the prophecy proved it. If she was a dragon her brother was a dragon, too.

She pulled back, tightly gripping him by the arms. "I'm really happy you're here, Kailas."

The prince's lips parted, but he had no idea what to say. He had just begun to smile, when the others came up behind them—dressed as warriors and armed to the teeth.

"Sorry to break up the touching moment," Tanya said loudly, elbowing her way in between the siblings to stand by Katerina's side. "But we don't want to be late to our own party."

"It sounded like they were really on to something." Cassiel flashed a grin, holding tight to her hand. "The only thing I heard was 'Cass was right'. Whatever the rest was—I fully approve."

The rest of the friends chuckled with quiet laughter, but before anyone could reply the desert rang with the call of a distant horn. They sobered immediately, looking up at the sky.

"Was that one of ours?" Katerina asked in confusion.

Aidan shook his head. "No...one of theirs."

The ground beneath them was trembling. Just faint vibrations at first, but before long the sand itself was dancing and they had trouble staying on their feet. They grabbed hold of each other for balance, but as quickly as it started the shaking suddenly stopped.

Katerina lifted her eyes to the mountains, then walked a few paces out into the sand. They'd camped right at the end of the range. Just around the corner lay the fields of Sorne.

Her friends followed beside her—the six of them walking slowly in a line. The rest of the army was just a few yards behind them, five entire kingdoms, but they didn't make a sound.

Katerina picked up the pace as she rounded the base of the mountain, then suddenly froze.

There were the fields, all right. A great stretching wasteland of cracked earth. On the other side loomed the Castle of Sorne, looking just as dark and uninviting as she'd imagined.

Dylan.

He was somewhere inside, trapped and alone. As she gazed up at the dark towers she imagined him standing at a window, gazing back down at her. The lost couple was finally reunited.

All that lay between them was the greatest demonic army she'd ever seen.

Seven hells.

It was too apt a profanity, she suddenly realized. Because it was as if each of the seven hells had suddenly opened, spilling all the wretched creatures inside straight onto the sand dunes.

Merrick had been right when he said they'd only seen a part of the Knight's forces. And Michael had been right when he'd predicted what was being held back.

Behind the rows of demons, behind the Kasi, and trolls, and goblins, and warlocks, and wraiths, and all the other things—too dark and terrible to look at closely—stood a row of creatures Katerina had never seen before. For a split second, she was convinced they couldn't be real. They were simply too large to exist in real life. They had to be statues. Then one of them tossed its head.

"...what are those?"

Beasts.

That's all Merrick had called them. Creatures that had been around as long as time, since the narrow straights that separated the realm were still covered by the sea. Creatures that had not been summoned from some distant land, but had clawed their way out of the earth on which they stood.

There were four of them in total, but Katerina didn't know why you'd ever need more than one. Each faintly resembled an animal you might find in the forest. A boar, a badger, a lion, and a bear. Easy enough, except each one stood a third as tall as the castle, and instead of fur they seemed to be covered in a thick coating of razor-tipped spikes. A pack of hell-hounds pawed the ground in front of them, looking like unruly toys in the shadow of their impossible size.

Kailas stared up at them a moment, then gave his sister a nudge. "Those are for us."

She started nodding automatically, then looked at him like he was crazy. "Wait—*what?!*"

As if to answer the boar took a step forward, crushing twelve Kasi beneath its foot. There was a mighty bellow, but she didn't think the beast noticed. It simply wanted to stretch.

"Dragon fire," Kailas said simply. "Once we shift, we'll be the only thing remotely close to their size. No other weapon could stand a chance."

The boar bellowed again and the lion snapped at it for silence. Katerina heard the clip of its teeth from over half a league away. Little drops of foam were falling from the bear's open jaws but, strangely enough, it was the badger that had her the most frightened.

"Oh...I don't know about that." She cast a hopeful look at the tall fae standing beside her, giving him a slight push forward at the same time. "Cass is a pretty good shot with that bow."

He tried to smile, but his eyes were grim. Clearly, now that he saw the army, the odds were exactly as terrible as he'd feared. His hand drifted lower, resting on Tanya's belly.

"Please don't fight," he said softly, knowing all the while it was no use. "Please get on a horse and ride back the way we came. Find somewhere safe to raise the baby."

She didn't argue with him, just simply smiled. "The safest place I know is with you." Their eyes met and she stretched up on her toes to give him a quick kiss. "Besides, I'm sure Kat has a plan. Right, princess?"

The girls exchanged a quick grin. It was the same thing the shapeshifter always asked when they found themselves in an impossible situation. Except, this time she wasn't far off base.

"Actually...come talk with me for a second."

They huddled together in a quick discussion. Tanya shook her head several times, then finally nodded at the end. A moment later, she slipped the ruby pendant's chain over her head.

One down, one to go.

"Cass." Katerina tugged at the fae's sleeve, unhooking Dylan's sword from her belt and holding it out in between them. "I want you to take it."

He looked down in surprise, tentatively lifting his hands to the blade. "Are you sure?"

She didn't want to part with it. But she didn't see how she could take it either.

"I have to shift," she explained as she gestured helplessly to the beasts. "I'd lose it."

He followed her gaze for a split second before his eyes drifted up to the castle. They flashed from window to window, as if he imagined the ranger standing there as well. A second later, he took the sword in a firm hand—giving it an automatic twirl before sheathing it in his belt.

"I'll hold on to it for you." He hesitated a moment, then glanced again at the castle. "I'll hold on to it for him."

Their eyes met for a fleeting moment, and even though he didn't know what was coming, even though he didn't know the steps she was ready to take, the fae made a silent request.

Find him. Bring him home.

Katerina nodded slowly, then focused her gaze straight ahead.

Behind her, people were saying quick goodbyes. Nothing overly sinister; most were infused with a false sense of optimism. *I'll see you after. Try to stay by my side.* No one was fooled, but everyone said them anyway. Michael and Petra shared a silent glance, then looked away with a smile.

As a stiff breeze blew back his hair, Aidan cast a secret glance at his brother. Merrick must have felt him looking, but his eyes never left the demonic horde. A single hand drifted up into the air and he spread his fingers. The vampires crouched with anticipation, ready to spring.

Then it started. There was no other warning than that.

With a fierce cry the two armies launched themselves towards each other, crashing together in the biggest collision of light and darkness the world had ever seen.

More than anything else, Katerina was stunned by the speed. In a flash, the battlefield had become a series of snapshots—splintered, fractured imagines racing one after another.

There was a flash of silver as a fae warrior decapitated a Ravren. A spray of crimson as a Kasi ripped off a shifter's arm. Vampires drifted in and out of the pictures like wisps of smoke, too fast to see them coming. Leaving a trail of demonic bodies in their wake.

The queen didn't understand how the rest of them could make sense of it. When Cassiel whipped out his sword—how did he manage to slice the warlock, as opposed to the Belarian wolf leaping next to him instead? It was all she could do to stay standing, to keep her balance against the ground. But a moment later, a ghoul knocked hard into her shoulder and she fell right off her feet.

All the breath rushed out of her the second she hit the ground, staring with wide eyes at the clouds of sand and blood misting up around the armies' feet. She tried to push herself back up but a swarm of goblins ran straight over top of her, each of them waving a miniature pike.

"Tan—"

She tried to call for the shifter, but got a mouthful of sand. She was about to try again, when a low growl echoed from somewhere over her shoulder. Even amidst the noise of the battle, she instinctively knew the growl was for her. A chill ran up her arms as she slowly turned around.

...only to see a giant hell hound staring back.

And not just any hell hound—

The queen let out a gasp as another hound peeled itself away from the battle, materializing by the first one's side. They shared a look of recognition before turning back to the dazed girl lying in the sand. A girl who was having a moment of recognition all of her own.

"Romulus," she croaked. "Remus."

Her brother's hounds—the ones Alwyn had used to work his dark magic, gifting them to the prince when he was only a boy. Those same hounds had chased her out of the castle, had hunted her through the forest, before they were finally driven away themselves.

But hell hounds never forget their prey. No matter how much time had passed.

They stalked forward as she scrambled back on her hands. Every time she tried to push to her feet, someone knocked her down again. Every time she tried to summon her fire, one of the hounds would growl and all that glowing magic would fizzle away.

Her mouth went dry, and a cold sweat drenched over her body. They were approaching from both sides now, lowering their heads to the ground as their lips pulled back in an anticipatory snarl. The one on the left licked its chops. The other was about to pounce.

But someone jumped in between them.

Kailas!

The prince lifted his sister with one hand, setting her back on her feet. In the same motion he turned to face his childhood pets, standing firmly in between them and their prize.

"Boys," he said softly.

Katerina stared at the back of his dark hair, still holding on to his wrist. She remembered how he used to say that around the castle. *Come on, boys* or *On your feet, boys—let's go for a hunt.* They blindly followed his every command. Most nights, they had slept at the foot of his bed.

Remus straightened slowly out of his crouch, staring at his old master. Romulus kept his aggressive position, but that vicious snarl left his eyes.

"You don't touch her," Kailas said quietly, pointing his sword at the demons rushing in from behind. "We fight them now."

The hounds actually glanced back before returning those blood-red eyes to the prince. A look of confusion passed over them. Remus looked at Katerina again and licked his lips.

"No," Kailas said sternly. "We fight *them*."

For a moment, none of them moved. For a moment, Katerina thought it had worked. Then the hounds leapt forward and a wave of liquid fire went flying from Kailas' hands.

They were dead before they hit the ground, falling in a smoldering pile at the prince's feet.

"...thanks," Katerina said breathlessly.

He jumped when she took his arm, still staring at their smoking bodies, then tore his gaze away. "Come on, we're running out of time."

In an act of mercy, the four giant beasts had been at the very back of the army—close to the castle, in case it required protection. It was a mercy in that it took them longer to reach the rest of them and they trampled many monsters and demons on their way.

But that luck was about to run out.

As Kailas and Katerina turned back to the battle, the badger and the lion had just reached the front lines. They tore straight through them without stopping, sending the bodies of a hundred men and shifters flying up in their wake. The lion stopped right in the middle, batting around its deadly paws and toying with its prey. The badger pressed its nose to the ground and kept racing forward, destroying anything and everything that stood in its way.

Katerina watched as a group of fae sprinted towards the mountain, flying halfway up the granite surface as if they had wings. In perfect unison, they lifted their bows and fired a volley of silver arrows—each one streaking directly towards the lion's face.

The arrows bounced off its hide. But they did get the beast's attention.

It released the witch it had been dangling, looking around for the source of the arrows. The second it spotted the fae it bounded through the camp, leaping up onto the cliffs beside them. The mountain shook so violently that most of them fell off. Those were the lucky ones. The ones who'd managed to remain were yanked into the air, thrashed around between a pair of deadly jaws until every spark of life had vanished from their bodies.

The whole thing happened in a matter of seconds. Brother and sister only had time to share a quick look before racing straight towards the beast across the sand. Cloaks and shoes kicked off as they ran. That heavy, suffocating armor fell behind them in the sand.

Then there was an explosion of fire and the Damaris twins took to the sky.

CASSIEL LIFTED HIS eyes just as the two dragons soared overhead. He'd been in the process of cutting down a cave troll who was terrorizing the Kreo camp, but paused long enough to flash them a quick smile. He was fighting with a sword in each hand. One was his. One was Dylan's.

Despite the many battles he'd fought over the years, this was undoubtedly the worst. If the fae had been worried about re-populating before, they would be in full crisis mode now. His people were dropping like flies. Having the most experience in the five kingdoms, they were usually the first to go charging into battle. In a battle such as this, they were usually the first to get cut down.

He ducked as the troll's spiked club swung towards him, then buried a warlock's halberd deep into its leg. There was a deafening cry as it toppled to its knees.

No sense in worrying about that now. He glimpsed Tanya fighting amidst the chaos, and his eyes sparked with a hint of pride. *No sense in worrying about that later either.*

He couldn't believe she was pregnant. No matter what monstrosity he found himself facing, the same four words kept echoing through his mind.

I'm pregnant, you stupid dumbass fairy!
An unlikely smile curved up his lips.

Eloquent as always. It was one of the reasons he'd fallen in love with her. That fiery disposition that contrasted so strongly against the some-times-forced regality of his own kind.

I wonder if it's a boy or a girl. He took out five Kasi demons, then launched himself off the back of a harpy to stab a hell hound in the back of the head. *I wonder if she's already thought of names—*

A hand closed around his arm and tugged sharply. A second later, he was on the ground.

He let out a gasp as he smashed into the sand, lifting his eyes in surprise. What he saw stole the breath right out of him. For a second, he was unable to move. That second cost him everything.

"No—"

But the Shien was already kneeling on top of him, crushing the life right out of him.

There was no fighting these creatures. He remembered the first time he'd told that to Dylan, how defiant the ranger had become. *You can fight anything*, he'd insisted. But he was wrong. Their strength was unmatched by anything on the planet. The trick was to not let them catch you in the first place. You could kill them in other ways, but if they laid a hand on you the game was done.

This one was no exception. It leaned forward, cracking half of his ribs.

He was dying, he could feel it. It had happened several times before. In an ambush on the road to Locksley, after the Midland Battles when his ship had sunk and he'd washed ashore. If the fairies hadn't found him, nursed him back to health, he would have died on that beach. But fairies couldn't come to the Dunes, and the warring armies were sweeping deeper into the fields.

There was a strange numbing sensation at the base of his neck. It terrified him and enraged him all at the same time. He fought even harder, thrashing around with desperate, violent cries.

But he was only hastening his own death.

Then, suddenly—he couldn't fight anymore. That numbness had taken hold and he sank with a silent breath into the cracked ground, gazing up at the Shien, waiting for death.

Strange, half-formed thoughts raced through his head.

The others would find him here. He'd dropped Dylan's sword somewhere on the ground. A shifter was getting stung to death by a giant centipede. He'd never get to see his baby's face.

But the battlefield wasn't yet deserted. A few people still remained.

Merrick flew past in a blur, then stopped just as suddenly—appearing perfectly motionless on the sand. His eyes drifted slowly between the Shien and the fae before turning rather grim. He knew a lost cause when he saw one. But the life of a fae was a precious thing to waste.

Cassiel stared in a daze, needing a moment to focus. What started as a look of hope paled to sudden dread. He froze when the vampire stepped towards him, staring up with quiet desperation.

"Merrick...don't—"

The vampire pounced.

There was a heartrending cry as he forced Cassiel's face to the side, sinking his teeth deep into the fae's neck. Streaks of crimson ran down his fair skin as he thrashed and struggled—pinned to death by one creature, drained dry by another.

He tried calling for help, tried desperately to escape. But Merrick drank deeply, shoving him down again with every attempt to rise. His vision was darkening. His hands fell limp in the sand.

Then, all at once...the vampire stopped.

Cassiel looked up in a drowsy sort of surprise. Even if the vampire had wanted to stop, he didn't think it was possible. Then again he was about to die, so it didn't really matter.

The two locked eyes for a split second. Then Merrick launched himself at the Shien.

...it moved.

The creature stumbled back, freeing Cassiel in the process. The fae froze for a moment, like he couldn't believe his eyes, then weakly began dragging himself backwards—out of the fight.

It was over quickly.

Merrick was careful not to let the creature lay hands on him, and it wasn't long before its head was flying away from its body. Decapitations seemed to be the vampire's signature style.

When he was finished, he turned around slowly—blood dripping from his fangs, eyes resting on the defenseless fae. There was a suspended moment where both of them wondered what the vampire was going to do. Then Merrick strode forward and reached towards him. Cassiel flinched, then stared up at the outstretched hand. After a moment, he took it.

"...thank you."

The second he was on his feet, Merrick deliberately pulled down the fae's hair—covering the bleeding wound and keeping it as a shield between them. Cassiel lowered his eyes as the world tilted and swayed, gripping the vampire's hand. A few moments before, he'd been flying across the sand, single-handedly decimating a cave troll. Now—he could scarcely stand.

Together, the two immortals began making their way across the desert. The battle raged on ahead of them, but they were stuck moving at a comically slow pace.

After a few minutes of silence, the fae shot the vampire a sideways glance. "Did you need to take so much?"

"No. Probably not."

Chapter 14

By the time Cassiel and Merrick caught up with the warring armies, the battle had reached a kind of swell. In a breathtaking coordinated attack, the Damaris dragons had turned the beasts against each other—dousing the badger in fire before tricking the lion into an attack.

They rolled in a blazing ball of flames across the sand, screaming in fury and destroying everything in their path. But with several strategic nips from the dragons, they hurled themselves in the opposite direction as the battle—out into the open dunes.

With two of the four monstrosities taken care of, they turned their attention to the boar. It had single-handedly destroyed the left flank of the royal army, and was currently trampling the coven of witches that was bravely standing in its way. The dragons shared a look then dove at the same time, streaking with wings of fire straight out of the sky. The beast rose up to meet them, pawing the air, and the game started anew. But that still left one beast unaccounted for.

The massive, rampaging bear.

With the dragons distracted, nothing could touch it. It tore completely unencumbered through the ranks of Belarian shifters, swatting them away like yapping little dogs. When it was finished with that, it lurched right into the middle of the royal forces and reared up on its hind legs, throwing back its head with a vicious, triumphant roar.

Katerina and Kailas were doing their best to outmaneuver the unruly boar. Michael and Petra had taken off after the lion and the badger into the desert. There was no one left to fight it.

But that didn't mean that some weren't still willing to try.

With a complete lack of fear Lysander looked up from the Ravren he was fighting and surveyed the beast, tilting his head back to see all the way to the top. A little smile danced around his lips as he killed the demon without looking and started walking towards it—dark hair blowing in a cloud around him, not a single weapon in his pale hands.

There was a chance the bear might not have even noticed him, but vampires have a way of making themselves known. With that same psychotic grin, he left the sand behind and started climbing straight up into its matted silver fur.

The creature roared in fury and tried to shake him off. It swung a mighty paw towards him, ripping into its own chest in the process. The vampire laughed as he was drenched in a shower of dark, brackish blood. He planted his feet in the wound and was about to climb higher.

When suddenly, that eternal luck ran out.

Merrick lifted his head like he'd been shocked, turning away from Cassiel mid-conversation to stare with wide eyes across the plain. He found Lysander a second later, just as the beast finished with him and dropped his body back to the ground.

The vampire froze where he stood, every muscle going rigid at the same time. For a prolonged moment, he simply stared. Then, slowly...he lifted his eyes to the bear.

"Can you stand?" he asked the fae in a low, soft voice.

Cassiel's eyes found the fallen vampire a second later. He tested his weight gingerly, then let go of Merrick's hand. The vampire left him there without another word, walking straight towards the beast through the middle of the rampaging crowd.

OF ALL THE TIMES TO have made a blood bond...

Aidan tightened his grip on the bronze javelin he was holding, then threw it with expert precision through the crowd. It hit right where he'd wanted—tearing through three goblins before piercing a crouched manticore in the heart.

He'd been in more fights than he could remember. In the three hundred years he'd been alive, those fights had pinned him against most every creature on the field of battle—in the demonic and the royal army alike.

But he'd never done it with the emotions of *four* people rattling around in his head.

At first, it was merely distracting.

He'd lift his hand to strike a blow—then look around suddenly as he felt a twinge of fear, or triumph, or pain. Somewhere on the battlefield one of his friends would be in a skirmish of their own, but the intensity of it was so strong he was having trouble telling the difference.

As the day progressed, it became more of a liability.

The fighting had grown dirtier, the stakes had grown higher, and the compounded reactions had left him in such a heightened emotional state he was having trouble steadying his hands.

Only after the fight had moved to the castle was he beginning to get a handle on things.

He sensed Katerina and Kailas as they flew overhead, but felt nothing other than an extreme amount of concentration as they communicated telepathically to coordinate each deadly attack. Tanya was a fiery whirlwind of emotion, but beneath all the exuberance lay a surprising layer of control.

There was a moment when Cassiel fell off his radar entirely, stopping the vampire's heart as he looked around in fear. But he reappeared a moment later, limping back towards the battle with a shadowy figure Aidan couldn't quite recognize in the sand.

He ducked suddenly as a ball of dark swirling light streaked his way and grazed the top of his shoulder. A whisper of pain was soon to follow, but fortunately it had only gotten his clothes and missed his skin. His eyes lifted to see a warlock standing motionless amidst the crowd. Another ball of shadow and flames was twirling on the tip of his finger.

The vampire watched him closely, centering his every attention. One had to be careful with warlocks. They might appear to be mortal men, but they'd been gifted with a dark and unpredictable power. He'd tasted that power before. He was not eager to do it again.

The man grinned cockily, pleased to have such a worthy opponent on the defensive. He'd been watching the vampire since the beginning of the battle, marveling in silent awe.

The ball bounced twice, then hovered in the air above his fingers—shimmering beneath the scorching desert sun. With nothing more than a whim, he could send it straight into the vampire's heart. But one had to be careful with vampires. They might appear pale and beautiful, but they were as vicious as they were wild—and nothing matched them for speed.

He would get a single throw. He would not get another.

Just do it already. Make up your mind.

Aidan tensed slightly, sinking down into an aggressive crouch.

He never saw the massive hell hound tearing its way toward him through the crowd. He never saw the beautiful girl that passed behind him, never felt the tips of her fingers brush his hair.

By the time she leapt at the hound, he was pouncing at the warlock.

The man collapsed in a pool of blood and death, calling out ancient curses as the light in his eyes flickered. Aidan retracted his fangs and let him bleed out instead, not wanting to sully himself by taking a drink. His dark hair swung into his eyes as his fingers slowly unlocked from their lethal grip on the man's shoulders. The ball of light had disintegrated the second it touched the sand.

He wanted to fight his way closer to the castle. The Knight had yet to make an appearance on the battlefield, and whatever decisive moment was coming it was sure to happen there. From what he could see, the rest of his friends were trying to do the same thing. No doubt, Katerina and Kailas would fly straight there after dispatching the—

A sudden chill shook him, freezing in his veins. Another chill and he leapt to his feet, lifting a hand to his chest. His eyes roved over the field of destruction, then abruptly stopped.

...no.

The people who saw it would forever remember when the beautiful vampire took on the hound. There wasn't an ounce of fear in her eyes as she raced towards it, flying across the sand like she'd been gifted a pair of dark wings. The two collided mid-air and rolled violently across the sand, ripping and biting, slashing out at each other with unspeakable power as the air around them misted with sprays of blood. There were several screams from the hound, but the vampire was perfectly silent. Even when its teeth sank into her neck, she never made a sound.

It died just as she fell back into the sand, landing in a graceful pile with her black hair whirling up around her. The world quieted as she stared up into the sky, wondering at what it might feel like, wondering if there was anything coming next.

Then, all at once...he was there.

"Maven!"

Her lips curved into a smile as she gazed up at Aidan's face. She'd always loved the way he said her name. It touched a part of her that no one else had ever been able to reach.

"My love, please—stay with me!"

His voice was shaking and his hands trembled as he gingerly lifted her off the sand. A river of blood streamed down her neck, and he let out a heartbreaking cry.

The next second, he was doing something she'd imagined for what seemed like the better part of her life. He was biting open his wrist, holding it gently to her lips.

"Drink," he gasped. "Please."

A stream of blood poured down his skin, trickling onto hers. The gesture he could never seem to reconcile. The bond he could never bring himself to make. Her body warmed and cooled at the same time. But she made no move to take it. She simply stared.

"Maven, open your mouth," he insisted, pulling at the corners. *"Please!"*

Their eyes met and she offered a tender smile. Then she leaned up and kissed him.

...then she died.

KATERINA WAS JUST FINISHING up with Kailas when she saw it happen. Even from a hundred feet up in the air, she heard the vampire's tortured cry. He was kneeling over Maven's body, sobbing. Clutching her to his chest like a doll. All around him, the battle raged on. But a new threat had just appeared on the horizon. A tall woman was sweeping towards him through the crowd.

Kailas saw it at the same time and shot her a quick look.

Go.

In a wave of crimson fire Katarina streaked towards the ground. But even as the air rushed up around her, even as her body melted back into human form—she knew she was too late.

Aidan didn't see Jazper until she'd grabbed him by the hair. He didn't notice the swarm of Carpathian warriors until they'd stampeded over half the field. He was still trying to catch his breath when she lifted him into the air, his feet dangling a foot off the ground.

"We meet again, my darling." She stroked his face with an affectionate smile before her eyes went cold. "Normally, I'd make a speech. But we're running low on time—"

He didn't have time to close his eyes before the blow fell. He was still reaching over his head for her wrist. But that deadly hand of hers flew fast and true, straight for his throat.

...until someone flashed in between.

There was a sudden cry as Jazper went spinning backwards, clutching at her face. A stain of blood dripped over her hand as she lifted her eyes in shock to see not one vampire, but two.

"You are magnificent," she breathed.

For perhaps the first time in his life, Merrick didn't smile.

"You took my baby brother's blood." His dark eyes glowed with quiet rage. "Didn't anyone ever tell you not to do that?"

Her smile faded ever so slightly, fading into something that looked almost sad. "There's no way I can convince you not to lose that pretty head, is there?"

Merrick bared his fangs.

"So be it." The wistful expression vanished as she swept her hair back, a thrill of anticipation dancing in her eyes. "I haven't had a good fight in years."

The vampire beckoned her forward. "Neither have I."

They vanished before anyone could try to stop them—moving too swiftly for mortal eyes to see. Aidan let out an involuntary shout for his brother, whirling around as he tried desperately to catch of glimpse of that dark hair. But Katerina caught his hand instead.

"We need to get to the castle." She cocked her head towards the raging battle, still holding on to his sleeve. "It's the only way to end this."

The arrival of the Carpathians had turned the tide in an already-grisly fight. The warriors of the five kingdoms were falling. Scattered demons were rallying back to the cause. It was only a matter of time before they were overcome entirely. Before the forces of darkness finally won.

Aidan searched a second more for Merrick, then turned back to the queen.

"What do you need me to do?"

As if on cue, Tanya appeared by their side. Cassiel was close behind her. Kailas and Serafina were on the other side of the sand field, but fighting their way through.

The shape-shifter reached into her shirt and handed Katerina the glowing pendant. The queen stared at it for a moment, then slipped the chain over her neck.

One hand gripped Aidan. The other pointed to the castle.

"I need to get through."

His dark eyes swept over the field of warriors in between them be-fore he set his jaw with a determined nod. A second later, he was swing-ing the queen over his back.

"Cover us," he commanded softly.

The others nodded, taking up position on either side.

They shared a fleeting glance, each of the friends together for one last time. Then with a wild cry, they took off running straight into the heart of the fight.

LOOKING BACK LATER, Katerina didn't know which moment stood out to her most. When Tanya leapt on the back of a hell hound to decimate the advancing Ravren army? When a trio of warlocks set the ground on fire, then Cassiel and Serafina lifted their hands and lit-erally made it rain? Perhaps it was when the three-headed dragon rose out of the castle and her twin brother exploded in a cloud of fire—tear-ing it straight out of the sky.

By the time Aidan dropped her on the steps of the castle there was no part of him that wasn't bleeding. She had miraculously arrived un-harmed. She suspected the two were related.

"That's it," he panted, falling to a knee in exhaustion. "We're here."

The stone doors were already open, as if the Knight had been wait-ing for her to arrive.

"Just give me a moment," Aidan continued, trying hard to catch his breath. "We'll go in together. There's no need for you to..."

But that's when he saw it—the Carpathian queen walking slowly through the crowd.

There was no sign of Merrick, only the blood dripping off her hands. Their eyes met for a suspended moment, then Aidan took a step away from Katerina—back into the sand.

"Go on without me," he murmured. "I'm staying here."

Her instinct was to warn him. Her instinct was to drag him inside and bolt the doors. But somehow, looking at his face, she didn't doubt that he'd be just fine.

She took off running a second later, the glowing ruby still gripped in her hand.

The castle was deserted. If the Knight had been expecting her, then he obviously wanted her to reach him as well. There wasn't a single other living soul as she sprinted up the winding stairwells, making her way slowly to the top. She didn't know where she was going. Only the fierce heat of the pendant seemed to light her way. Her feet flew down corridor after corridor, but some abstract impulse made her stop suddenly. She doubled backwards, pushed open a door...

...then froze dead still.

Dylan was standing in the middle of an empty throne room. A dagger was in one hand. The crown was in the other. She took a step towards him, then saw the Knight standing by his side.

"The star-crossed lovers are reunited again." Nathaniel clapped his hands with a beaming smile. "What a fitting end to our story."

Katerina tried to step closer, but the second she moved Dylan lifted the dagger in his hand.

The message was simple: attack and die.

She'd seen him throw a knife enough times to trust his aim.

"So this is what you wanted?" she asked, her voice echoing loudly in the chilling quiet of the room. "I hand you the stone or he kills me?"

The Knight smiled again, taking a step closer. "Oh no, sweetheart. Nothing so barbaric as that." He cocked his head to the side, surveying her with a pair of glittering eyes. "You hand me the stone or he kills himself."

In a flash Dylan turned the dagger inward, pressing the lethal blade to the skin just above his heart. His hands were shaking but his eyes were blank, as if he'd somehow fallen asleep.

"If you're so sure of yourself, let him go," Katerina answered quietly. If the man could control him, perhaps the man could free him as well. "You have no need for him anymore."

"Oh, but I enjoy this," he parried. "Dylan, give us a little demonstration."

Without hesitation, the ranger pressed the blade into his skin. A trickle of blood was soon to follow, spattering loudly onto the floor.

Katerina took a compulsive step forward then froze, gritting her teeth. "To be a king, your subjects must have free will. Otherwise it's—"

"They will serve just the same." The knight stepped even closer, savoring every moment of the twisted little game. With a grin he pressed another knife into Dylan's hand, directing it this time towards Katerina. "Now her. Just a scratch, mind you. Nothing serious."

The queen sucked in a quick breath as Dylan lifted his hand. The tendons tightened as his eyes zeroed in on her sleeve. But instead of letting it go, he froze.

"I-I can't..." His voice was distant and strange, as if he was speaking from somewhere very far away. "I can't be sure I wouldn't miss."

The Knight's smile faltered as he took a step forward. In a seemingly casual gesture he wrapped an arm around the ranger's shoulder, only to press his fingers straight into the wound.

"Just a scratch, mind you." He repeated his exact words. "Nothing serious."

A strange expression flashed across Dylan's face, like he was touching his hand to an open flame. He nodded quickly, raising the dagger once more. But it dropped to the floor with a clatter.

Katerina sensed her opening and took it.

"I love you," she said softly. "You remember that, right?"

His blue eyes flashed to hers, tightening like he was in physical pain. She took a little step closer. Ignoring the Knight. Ignoring the dagger. Focused only on the ranger who'd won her heart.

"Before we met, I wanted adventure," she continued. "When you asked me to leave all that behind, to run away with you, I didn't know what to say. I'd always wanted the adventure."

A step closer. Then another step after that.

"Do you know what I want now?"

His lips parted uncertainly, but the Knight stepped angrily in between.

"Enough!" He shoved the ranger forward, stumbling onto the stone. "I haven't waited so long to listen to such things. Kill the girl. Bring me the stone."

Dylan took a step closer, too, then paused—staring at Katerina. A war of emotions was dancing behind his eyes. For a moment, it looked strong enough to tear him in two.

But then—

"What do you want now?" he whispered.

Her eyes warmed with a glow.

"I want to live in that farmhouse with you."

There are certain moments in every fairytale that defy expectation. Moments that seem so unlikely, they baffle the reader for years to come. If Katerina had been reading this story as a child, she might have said this was one of those moments. She might have said the invocation of a quiet future living in a farmhouse couldn't possibly be enough to break the spell.

But she would have been wrong. Because that's the thing about fairytales. Some fairytales went farther than just having a happily ever after. Some fairytales actually came true.

Dylan threw her the crown.

She caught it, and in the same motion slipped in the ruby stone.

And the rest, they say, is history...

Epilogue

Katerina walked slowly through the forest, her long dress trailing over a bed of moss and leaves. It was one of those perfect balmy summer evenings, when the air had just enough bite to remind you that the winds of autumn would soon be rustling through the trees.

She paused briefly at a fork in the river then turned suddenly to the left, winding her way through a grove of jasmine and maple until she found what she was looking for.

A man kneeling by himself at the base of a tree.

Most days, he would have heard her coming. Most days, he would have felt her decide to find him—even before she was aware of it herself. But not today. Today, he was in a world all his own. One hand resting lightly on the dirt, his dark eyes a thousand miles away.

He jumped slightly when she knelt beside him, resting a hand on his arm.

"What are you doing here? Shouldn't you be..." he trailed off helplessly as she stared back with a patient smile. "I'm sorry, I must have-I must have lost track of time."

Together, they lowered their eyes to the unmarked grave.

A profound change had come over Aidan on the steps of the castle, a kind of transformation that no one watching would ever be able to explain. The second he saw his brother's blood, a kind of trance had taken over—propelling him back into the battle and across the sand.

He didn't stop when he reached Jazper. He barely gave her a second glance. His hand shot out when they crossed paths, then he continued moving onward...holding her beating heart.

He had been too late to save his brother. But Merrick did have one final request.

"Here." With every bit of strength he had left Merrick lifted a hand between them, offering it to his little brother. "Drink."

Aidan stared down in shock, tears streaming from his eyes.

"But you don't—"

"Do this for me," Merrick insisted softly. A rush of pain shook through him and he pulled in a faltering breath. "I want-I want to know what it's like."

With trembling hands, Aidan took his brother's wrist and pressed it to his lips. A rush of feeling swept over him and he let out a breathless gasp. Their eyes met for a fleeting moment; one openly weeping, one looking strangely calm. Then the vampire closed his eyes and the feeling faded.

The first and last blood bond that Merrick Dorsett would ever make.

"You were right," Aidan said softly, staring down at the grave. "He really did love me."

Katerina gave his hand a gentle squeeze. "Yes, he did."

They knelt there for a while in silence, each thinking of things that would take them decades to understand. Then Katerina pushed to her feet, reaching for Aidan.

"You know what I don't want to do today? Spend time at a grave."

Aidan took her hand with a smile, eyes twinkling as he played along. "What do you want to do today?"

Her face lit up as a summer breeze danced around her long white dress. "I want to get married."

THE MUSIC HAD ALREADY started by the time the queen and the vampire arrived in the garden.

Under the fierce glare of the wedding planner Aidan adjusted her dress, smoothed down her hair, then ducked under the veil to give her a quick kiss on the cheek.

"If you want to run—just give me a signal," he whispered. "You invited a vampire to your wedding. I'll just start massacring the guests."

She bit her lip with a grin. "I'd be insulted if you didn't."

Then the music swelled and she turned away.

Another man was waiting at the end of the aisle. Hands folded in front of him, sword hanging by his side. Watching her every movement with a pair of twinkling blue eyes.

Her heart leapt in her chest as she started walking towards him.

It was, without a doubt, the strangest royal wedding the five kingdoms had ever seen.

In the audience there were shifters and fae, men and witches, nymphs and dwarves—even a pixie or two. A trio of brightly-colored fairies hovered above the archway, waving excitedly as she glided down the aisle. Bernard the giant stood in the far corner, sobbing loudly, bucket-sized tears pouring from his eyes.

But those were just her friends. Her family was there as well.

Cassiel had returned only a few nights before from the city of Taviel, where restorations were well under way. He'd led what was left of his people there on foot—hiking through the ancient forest until they cleared the trees and saw the crumbling remains.

It had been an emotional moment. Several of the people standing with him looked like they were ready to go back. But before they could turn around, the strangest thing happened.

The Lithian heron flew from Cassiel's shoulder and alighted on the stone.

The city that had a thousand names was given a few more.

It was a city rebuilt. A hope rekindled. A people reborn.

And what better way to christen a new city than to give it a new queen?

Tanya was sitting by Cassiel's side—a delicate silver crown woven into her cinnamon hair.

The mortal maiden and immortal warrior had no plan for how they would stay together when the dust of the final battle finally fell. But as Serafina said once before, the fates are never intentionally cruel. It turned out the prophecy that united them had done a bit more.

The moment the crown and the stone came together...a new era had begun.

A kind of mist rolled out of the castle—a shimmering light that fell on the five friends and each faithful subject of their kingdoms. The 'grace', the promised protection, had come just in the nick of time. The demons had been driven away. The castle was reduced to ruins.

And the Red Knight himself?

The man finally got the death that was promised to him over five hundred years before. But instead of meeting his end in Laurelwood, his heart was pierced with the tip of Dylan's sword.

They had thought it was enough. The forces of darkness were defeated. The prophecy was complete. But as it turned out, the protection meant more than just success in battle.

It also came with the promise of eternal life.

Of course, with every new beginning something old must end.

For the first time in hundreds of years, Michael and Petra began to age. The younger generation had been horrified—Dylan had instinctively offered to smash the stone—but the siblings embraced the change with open arms. Too long had they roamed about the five kingdoms. Too long had they been separated from their beloved Eliea. It was time for it to finish. It was time for peace.

They were sitting in the garden as well—streaked with grey and beaming with happiness as the young queen swept down the aisle. Tanya was settled right in front of them and Cassiel was by her side—a little white-haired boy sitting in his lap.

The couple was settling into parenthood nicely. Milk and story time after dinner, with secret rides on the dragon whenever Leonor was away.

The day they'd returned to the High Kingdom Cassiel had raced onto the lawn, yelling angrily as Dylan and the boy sparred with swords. Furious not that the ranger had given the toddler a blade, but that he was teaching him what the fae called inferior technique.

Kailas and Serafina were sitting right next to them, a ring of white diamonds sparling on her finger. Aidan had changed into a dark suit, now leaning against a pillar with that twinkling smile.

It was everything the queen could have ever wanted. As if all those fairytales she and Kailas had read as children had suddenly come to life.

She reached Dylan at the end of the aisle and slowly took his hands.

"Hey stranger," he murmured. "You ready for this?"

The ruby pendant glowed on her neck.

"I could be persuaded."

I've been ready all my life.

The royal officiant droned on and on as they stood there staring at each other. Every now and then, she'd squeeze his hands. Every now and then, he'd give her a little wink.

When the ceremony was finally finished, he lifted the veil—his face softening with a tender smile as he stared down into her eyes.

"No more adventures, huh?"

He pressed a sweet kiss to her lips, one that promised many more to come.

"Oh, I don't know about that." Her eyes twinkled with the promise of an eternal future as he slipped the ring onto her finger. "I have a feeling the adventure's only begun..."

THE END

Note from Author:

I hope you've enjoyed the series as much as I have created it! I also hope, like me, you aren't ready to say good-bye to these loveable characters!

If you are up for a new journey, come join me in the OMEGA QUEEN series and see what happens after the ancient prophecy has been fulfilled!

Discipline Blurb:

She will die to protect those who are hers.

... Be careful who you trust.
Even the devil was once an angel.

The Queen's Alpha Series

Eternal

Everlasting

Unceasing

Evermore

Forever

Boundless

Prophecy

Protected

Foretelling

Revelation

Betrayal

Resolved

The Omega Queen Series

Discipline
Bravery
Courage
Conquer
Strength
Validation

Find W.J. May

Website:
http://www.wanitamay.yolasite.com
Facebook:
https://www.facebook.com/pages/Author-WJ-May-FAN-PAGE/
141170442608149
Newsletter:
SIGN UP FOR W.J. May's Newsletter to find out about new releases,
updates, cover reveals and even freebies!
http://eepurl.com/97aYf

More books by W.J. May

The Chronicles of Kerrigan

Book I - *Rae of Hope* is FREE!
Book Trailer:
http://www.youtube.com/watch?v=gILAwXxx8MU
Book II - *Dark Nebula*
Book Trailer:
http://www.youtube.com/watch?v=Ca24STi_bFM
Book III - *House of Cards*
Book IV - *Royal Tea*
Book V - *Under Fire*
Book VI - *End in Sight*
Book VII – *Hidden Darkness*
Book VIII – *Twisted Together*
Book IX – *Mark of Fate*
Book X – *Strength & Power*
Book XI – *Last One Standing*
BOOK XII – *Rae of Light*

PREQUEL –
Christmas Before the Magic

Question the Darkness
Into the Darkness
Fight the Darkness
Alone the Darkness
Lost the Darkness

SEQUEL –
    Matter of Time
    Time Piece
    Second Chance
    Glitch in Time
    Our Time
    Precious Time

Hidden Secrets Saga:
Download Seventh Mark part 1 For FREE
Book Trailer:
http://www.youtube.com/watch?v=Y-_vVYC1gvo

Like most teenagers, Rouge is trying to figure out who she is and what she wants to be. With little knowledge about her past, she has questions but has never tried to find the answers. Everything changes when she befriends a strangely intoxicating family. Siblings Grace and Michael, appear to have secrets which seem connected to Rouge. Her hunch is confirmed when a horrible incident occurs at an outdoor party. Rouge may be the only one who can find the answer.

An ancient journal, a Sioghra necklace and a special mark force life-altering decisions for a girl who grew up unprepared to fight for her life or others.

All secrets have a cost and Rouge's determination to find the truth can only lead to trouble...or something even more sinister.

RADIUM HALOS - THE SENSELESS SERIES
Book 1 is FREE

Everyone needs to be a hero at one point in their life.

The small town of Elliot Lake will never be the same again.

Caught in a sudden thunderstorm, Zoe, a high school senior from Elliot Lake, and five of her friends take shelter in an abandoned uranium mine. Over the next few days, Zoe's hearing sharpens drastically, beyond what any normal human being can detect. She tells her friends, only to learn that four others have an increased sense as well. Only Kieran, the new boy from Scotland, isn't affected.

Fashioning themselves into superheroes, the group tries to stop the strange occurrences happening in their little town. Muggings, break-ins, disappearances, and murder begin to hit too close to home. It leads the team to think someone knows about their secret - someone who wants them all dead.

An incredulous group of heroes. A traitor in the midst. Some dreams are written in blood.

Courage Runs Red
The Blood Red Series
Book 1 is FREE
WHAT IF COURAGE WAS your only option?

When Kallie lands a college interview with the city's new hot-shot police officer, she has no idea everything in her life is about to change. The detective is young, handsome and seems to have an unnatural ability to stop the increasing local crime rate. Detective Liam's particular interest in Kallie sends her heart and head stumbling over each other.

When a raging blood feud between vampires spills into her home, Kallie gets caught in the middle. Torn between love and family loyalty she must find the courage to fight what she fears the most and possibly risk everything, even if it means dying for those she loves.

Daughter of Darkness - Victoria
Only Death Could Stop Her Now
The Daughters of Darkness is a series of female heroines who may or may not know each other, but all have the same father, Vlad Montour.
Victoria is a Hunter Vampire

Don't miss out!

Visit the website below and you can sign up to receive emails whenever W.J. May publishes a new book. There's no charge and no obligation.

https://books2read.com/r/B-A-SSF-OENX

BOOKS 2 READ

Connecting independent readers to independent writers.

Did you love *Resolved*? Then you should read *School of Potential* by
W.J. May!

*USA Today Bestselling author, W.J. May brings you a continuation of the
international bestselling series, The Chronicles of Kerrigan! Come back
and enjoy the famous characters, or step into the series right here. You
won't be disappointed!*

How do you save the world, when it's already been saved?

Eighteen-year-old Aria was supposed to have it all. A tight-knit circle of friends, a loving family, and a magical tatu on her lower back that
gave her every superpower under the sun. When it came to the battle
between good and evil, she was ready to do her part. There was just one
little problem.

...good had already won.

Trapped beneath their parents' legacy, Aria and her friends find
themselves restlessly pacing the halls of Guilder University, desperate

to come into their powers, desperate for whatever comes next. The months blend together, each more monotonous than the next, until one day, no different than any other, a mysterious stranger comes to school.

Determined to uncover his secrets and driven by a fierce need to prove themselves, the new gang does whatever it takes to show the rest of the world they're ready. But that readiness comes at a cost.

Will it be a price they're willing to pay?

Kerrigan Kids
School of Potential
Myths of Magic
Kith & Kin
Playing With Power
Line of Ancestry
Descent of Hope
Read more at www.wjmaybooks.com.

Also by W.J. May

Bit-Lit Series
Lost Vampire
Cost of Blood
Price of Death

Blood Red Series
Courage Runs Red
The Night Watch
Marked by Courage
Forever Night
The Other Side of Fear

Daughters of Darkness: Victoria's Journey
Victoria
Huntress
Coveted (A Vampire & Paranormal Romance)
Twisted
Daughter of Darkness - Victoria - Box Set

Hidden Secrets Saga
Seventh Mark - Part 1
Seventh Mark - Part 2
Marked By Destiny
Compelled
Fate's Intervention
Chosen Three
The Hidden Secrets Saga: The Complete Series

Kerrigan Chronicles
Stopping Time
A Passage of Time
Ticking Clock
Secrets in Time
Time in the City
Ultimate Future

Mending Magic Series
Lost Souls
Illusion of Power
Challenging the Dark
Castle of Power

Paranormal Huntress Series
Never Look Back
Coven Master

Alpha's Permission
Blood Bonding
Oracle of Nightmares
Shadows in the Night
Paranormal Huntress BOX SET #1-3

Prophecy Series
Only the Beginning
White Winter
Secrets of Destiny

The Chronicles of Kerrigan
Rae of Hope
Dark Nebula
House of Cards
Royal Tea
Under Fire
End in Sight
Hidden Darkness
Twisted Together
Mark of Fate
Strength & Power
Last One Standing
Rae of Light
The Chronicles of Kerrigan Box Set Books # 1 - 6

The Chronicles of Kerrigan: Gabriel
Living in the Past

Present For Today
Staring at the Future

The Chronicles of Kerrigan Prequel
Christmas Before the Magic
Question the Darkness
Into the Darkness
Fight the Darkness
Alone in the Darkness
Lost in Darkness
The Chronicles of Kerrigan Prequel Series Books #1-3

The Chronicles of Kerrigan Sequel
A Matter of Time
Time Piece
Second Chance
Glitch in Time
Our Time
Precious Time

The Hidden Secrets Saga
Seventh Mark (part 1 & 2)

The Kerrigan Kids
School of Potential

Forest of the Forbidden
Arcane Forest: A Fantasy Anthology
The First Fantasy Box Set

Watch for more at www.wjmaybooks.com.

About the Author

About W.J. May

Welcome to USA TODAY BESTSELLING author W.J. May's Page! SIGN UP for W.J. May's Newsletter to find out about new releases, updates, cover reveals and even freebies! http://eepurl.com/97aYf

Website: http://www.wjmaybooks.com

Facebook: http://www.facebook.com/pages/Author-WJ-May-FAN-PAGE/141170442608149?ref=hl *Please feel free to connect with me and share your comments. I love connecting with my readers.* W.J. May grew up in the fruit belt of Ontario. Crazy-happy childhood, she always has had a vivid imagination and loads of energy. After her father passed away in 2008, from a six-year battle with cancer (which she still believes he won the fight against), she began to write again. A passion she'd loved for years, but realized life was too short to keep putting it off. She is a writer of Young Adult, Fantasy Fiction and where ever else her little muses take her.

Read more at www.wjmaybooks.com.